SIX
O'CLOCK
TALES

EGMONT

First published in Great Britain 1942 by Methuen & Co Ltd
Dean edition first published 1991
Mammoth edition first published 1993
This edition published 2008
by Egmont UK Limited
239 Kensington High Street
London W8 6SA

Text trademark and copyright © 1942 Chorion Rights Limited.
All rights reserved.
Cover copyright © 2008 Teresa Murfin

ISBN 978 1 4052 3973 8

1 3 5 7 9 10 8 6 4 2

www.egmont.co.uk

A CIP catalogue record for this title is available from the British Library

Printed and bound in Great Britain by the CPI Group

CONTENTS

When the Moon Fell Down!

One evening, when the moon was full and shone out in a cloudy sky, Prickles the Hedgehog went out to look for a beetle or two for his dinner. When he was under a chestnut tree a large chestnut fell down on his back and made him jump in fright. At the same moment the moon disappeared behind a cloud.

'Ooh!' cried Prickles at once. 'The moon fell down on my back! Ooh! I felt it! It's fallen out of the sky! I must tell Frisky the Squirrel.'

He found Frisky and told him. 'The moon has fallen out of the sky!' he said. 'It hit my back. I felt it. What shall we do?'

Frisky was excited. 'We must tell Hoo-Hoo the Brown Owl,' he said. So they went to where Hoo-Hoo was sitting on a branch and told him.

'The moon has fallen out of the sky!' said Frisky the Squirrel. 'It hit Prickles on the back. He felt it. What shall we do?'

Hoo-Hoo was astonished. He looked up into

the cloudy sky, but he could certainly see no moon there.

'We must tell Sly-One the Stoat,' he said. So all three set off to the barn where Sly-One was watching for mice.

'Sly-One, listen!' cried Hoo-Hoo. 'The moon has fallen out of the sky! It hit Prickles on the back, he felt it. What shall we do?'

Sly-One could hardly believe his ears. He jumped up excitedly. 'We must tell Velvety the Mole,' he said. So they all hurried off to where Velvety was making a big tunnel in the field.

'Listen, Velvety!' cried Sly-One. 'The moon has fallen out of the sky! It hit Prickles on the back. He felt it. What shall we do?'

'Why, go and find it, of course!' said Velvety at once. So they all ran to the place where Prickles had felt certain that the moon had fallen on his back, and began to hunt about.

The wind blew a little, and a few more chestnuts fell down. Bump! One hit Frisky the Squirrel on the nose. Bump! Another hit Sly-One the Stoat on his arched back. Bump! A third hit Hoo-Hoo the Owl on his beak.

'Why, the chestnuts are falling!' cried Frisky, picking one up and nibbling it. 'It must have been a chestnut you felt, Prickles. What a silly you are!'

Prickles didn't like being called silly. He stood all his spines up on end at once. 'I tell you, it was the moon!' he said crossly. 'Don't I know the difference between the moon and a chestnut?'

And dear me, at that very moment the moon sailed out from behind a cloud and lit up the wood with its bright silvery light!

'Ho, ho!' laughed all the creatures. 'There's the moon in the sky, after all. So you *didn't* know the difference between the moon and a chestnut! Funny old Prickles!'

But Prickles wasn't there! He had crept away to hide in a ditch, quite ashamed of himself. Poor old hedgehog!

Jean's Little Thrush

Jean had a nice little garden at school. She was very proud of it because she had three rose trees in it, and a border of blue lobelia and white sweet alyssum. The other children had sown seeds of candytuft, poppies, nasturtiums and clarkia, but Jean's was the only garden with rose trees.

She had saved up her money and bought them herself, because she loved roses. There was a tree that would bear red roses, one that would bear pink ones and the third one was yellow. Jean hoped to be able to have a fine bowlful of roses for her schoolroom, and a bunch to take home to her mother.

The head mistress of the school called the little gardeners to her one day and promised a prize for the best-kept garden with the loveliest flowers. Jean did hope hers would be the best, and every day she went to weed it and water her plants, which were growing very well.

One day when she was weeding her garden she heard a loud squeaking noise not far off. It sounded like a gate creaking and Jean wondered what it was. She looked all round but could not see anything at all. The noise still went on so she ran off to find out what it was.

It wasn't long before she discovered what was making the noise. It was a small baby thrush! It sat on the ground beneath a flowering lilac and squeaked with fright. Nearby was the mother thrush making little comforting noises. Jean looked at the frightened baby bird.

'It's too small to fly,' she thought. 'It must have fallen out of its nest. I wonder where the nest is?'

She looked up into the lilac bush. It wasn't there. She looked into the next tree, a chestnut, big and spreading – and there, set neatly in the fork of three small branches she spied a thrush's nest! Over the edge of it peeped a brown head – another baby thrush!

'There!' said Jean. 'I was right! This little thing has tumbled out of its nest. Oh dear, what shall I do? I can't possibly climb up there.'

She stood there, thinking. The baby thrush at her feet kept on squeaking. Jean felt sure a cat would hear it soon if it didn't keep quiet. But it didn't know anything about cats. It just thought that if it went on squeaking someone or something would come to its help.

'I know!' said Jean, at last. 'I'll get the little ladder that Miss Brown keeps in the shed. Then I can climb up and put the bird back quite easily.'

So off she went. She soon got the ladder, and although it was rather heavy it wasn't long before she had set it up against the chestnut tree. She picked the baby thrush up very carefully in her hand and then climbed up the ladder. The mother thrush flew round her as she carried the squeaking bird, and cried out in fear, afraid that Jean was going to harm her little bird.

Carefully Jean put the little thrush into the nest and then climbed down the ladder again.

'Stay in your nest till you are big enough to fly properly!' she called to the baby thrush. 'I might not be near if you fall out again.'

She put the ladder back and went on with her gardening, glad that the little thrush had stopped its frightened squeaking.

Soon after that Jean caught a cold and had to stay at home for a week. When she came back, anxious to look at her garden, what a shock she got! The leaves of her rose trees were all stuck together, and when she pulled them apart she found little green caterpillars all over the trees! They were eating great holes in the leaves, and were even starting to nibble at the nice new rosebuds.

Jean stared at the spoilt rose trees with tears in her eyes. How unlucky that the caterpillars should have come just the week she was away! In a fortnight's time the head mistress, Miss Brown, was going to look at the school gardens and give the prize. Unless Jean could get rid of all the caterpillars in a short time, her rose trees would certainly not be worth looking at!

Then she saw a speckled thrush come hopping over the lawn, followed by three wobbly baby thrushes! The mother thrush was teaching them to look for food. She hopped over to Jean's garden and put her head on one side, looking up into the rose trees. Then, with a quick peck she snapped at a green caterpillar, and, hopping back to her three babies, she popped it quickly into one of their open mouths. Jean was delighted!

'Oh, do take away all the caterpillars that are spoiling my rose trees!' she begged the thrush.

'Trilla-trilla, pretty pretty, trilla!' said the

thrush at once, which Jean was sure meant: 'I will! You once saved one of my babies, and now I will do your garden a good turn!'

The school bell rang and Jean ran in to her class. For the next two or three days the mother thrush came to her little garden a dozen times a day and very soon there was not a caterpillar left!

Jean was so pleased. She carefully picked off all the half-eaten leaves and nipped off the spoilt buds. There was over a week before the head mistress was going to judge the school gardens. Perhaps there would be a chance for Jean after all!

You should have seen Jean's rose trees in a week's time! They had put out nice fresh leaves and every tree had some beautiful roses blooming. The sweet alyssum and the blue lobelia round the little bed were all blossoming gaily, and there wasn't a weed to be seen.

The head mistress looked at all the gardens, but when she came to Jean's she stopped and admired it very much.

'Yours is beautiful,' she said to the proud little girl. 'There isn't a weed to be seen, and your rose trees are lovely. I was afraid they would all be eaten by some caterpillars I saw on them a fortnight ago.'

'Oh, a kind thrush came and ate them all,' said Jean.

'And who was the kind little girl who did a good turn to a baby thrush?' asked Miss Brown. 'I saw all you did from my window, Jean. Well, you were kind to the thrush, the thrush returned your kindness and ate your caterpillars – and now I shall give you the prize for the best and prettiest garden in the school! You deserve it!'

Everyone cheered, and Jean walked proudly up to take the set of fine garden tools that Miss Brown held out to her. And just as she was taking them a thrush up in the trees began to sing a loud, glad song.

'There's your friend the thrush cheering you!' said Miss Brown. And I shouldn't be surprised if it was, would you?

You Can't Please Everybody!

Flip and Flap were two jolly gnomes who tried to please everyone. But once they tried too often, as you shall hear!

It happened one day that they wanted to go to market to fetch some potatoes in their barrow and Flap thought it would be a good idea to take with them a sack of apples to sell. So they fetched the big wheelbarrow and filled a sack full of their best apples. Then they set off.

Now Flip was very tall and thin and Flap was very short and stout, so they looked an odd pair. Flip wheeled the barrow and Flap took the sack of apples on his fat shoulder. It was a hot day and the road to the market was a long one. Many people were going to market that day, and some of them stared laughingly at the two gnomes.

'Look at that little fat one carrying the sack!' cried a big brownie, pointing his long finger at Flap. 'What foolish gnomes they are! Why don't they put the sack in the barrow and wheel it?

Then it need not be carried!'

'Dear me!' said Flip, stopping and looking at Flap. 'We might have thought of that, Flap. Put the sack of apples in the barrow and I can easily wheel it.'

So Flap thankfully put the sack into the barrow and walked on his way, glad to be rid of his load. But tall, thin Flip found the barrow rather heavy to push and every now and again he gave a little groan. Some pixies passing by heard him and they stopped and pointed their fingers at fat Flap, swinging along by himself, whistling.

'Look at that strong, fat gnome selfishly walking by himself, letting his poor thin brother push that heavy barrow!' they cried. 'For shame! He ought to push the barrow himself!'

The gnomes stopped and Flap went very red. He took the handles of the barrow from Flip at once.

'Better let me push the barrow, Flip,' he said. 'I don't want people to think I am selfish, for I am much too fond of you to be unkind. You walk and I will take the barrow.'

So tall, thin Flip walked beside the barrow whistling gaily, while short, fat Flap pushed it. The sun was very hot indeed and soon Flap panted and puffed with the heat. He pushed the barrow along, and felt little drops of water running down his face, because he was so hot.

A large gnome and his wife came jogging up on their donkey and the wife pointed her finger at Flip in disgust.

'Look, husband,' she said, 'do you see that tall gnome there walking by his poor little brother who is working himself to death pushing that heavy barrow? For shame! Why doesn't he help him? Surely he could give him a hand?'

Then it was Flip's turn to go red. The tall gnome stopped and looked at Flap, who was still puffing and panting as he pushed the barrow.

'Look here!' said Flip. 'Hadn't we better push the barrow together, Flap? You can take one handle and I can take the other. Then everyone can see we are helping one another.'

So Flap took the right handle of the barrow and Flip took the left handle, and off they went again down the road.

Very soon a big party of pixies rattled by in a wagon, and when they saw the two gnomes both pushing the one wheelbarrow they screamed with laughter and pointed their small fingers at them in scorn.

'Look! Look! Those gnomes are so weak and

feeble that it needs both of them to push one barrow! Oh, what a funny sight! Poor things! They ought to eat lots of eggs and butter to get up their strength. Then it wouldn't need two of them to push one small barrow!'

The gnomes put down the barrow with a bang and stared angrily after the cheeky pixies.

'*Well!*' said Flap, snorting down his nose in rage. 'We can't seem to please anybody this morning! What are we to do now?'

'Well, it's no use one of us carrying the apples and the other wheeling the barrow,' said Flap, 'because we were laughed at for that.'

'And it's no good you wheeling the barrow alone or me wheeling it either,' said Flap gloomily, 'because people think we're selfish then.'

'And they think we're poor, weak things if we wheel it together,' said Flip. 'But wait – *I* know what we'll do, Flap! You carry the barrow over your shoulder, and *I'll* carry the sack of apples! Then we shall neither of us be called stupid, selfish or feeble. Isn't that a good idea?'

'Fine!' said Flap, and he hoisted the barrow on to his head. The weight of it bent him over and he couldn't see where he was going, so he told Flip to walk in front of him and guide him.

Flip went in front and together they made their way to the market.

The road began to get very crowded, and pigs, hens and ducks were all over the place. Suddenly a little pig ran between Flip's long legs and over he went with the bag of apples. They rolled all over the road and the pigs gobbled them up at once! Then Flap fell over Flip and down came the barrow, crash! Its wheel broke in half and both the handles were cracked.

'My goodness me!' said Flap, sitting up and looking in dismay at the pigs gobbling the apples and at his broken barrow. 'Look at that, Flip! This is what comes of trying to please everybody! *Next* time we will please ourselves!'

And I really think it would be better if they did, don't you?

The King of the Trains

Malcolm had a big red engine for his birthday.
You should have seen it! It was the biggest toy
engine he had ever seen, so big that Malcolm
and his sister Janet could easily get into the back
of it and sit there together!

Malcolm had a rope tied round the red funnel
and he used to pull Janet round the garden in
the engine. Then he would have *his* turn at
riding and Janet would pull. It was great fun.

One day a very strange thing happened. The
children were in the garden and had squeezed
themselves into the engine together. 'I wish the
engine would go off by itself and take us along,'
said Malcolm.

Just as he said that the children heard a sound
in the distance like the loud whistle of an
engine. At once their own engine gave a start as
though it had heard. Then, to the children's
enormous surprise, it began to puff away down
the garden path!

Yes! It really puffed! Smoke came out of the funnel, and it went faster and faster down the path! It was a very strange and peculiar thing!

'Goodness!' said Malcolm in astonishment. 'Whatever's happening?'

'Hadn't we better get out?' asked Janet, but the engine was now going much too fast for them to get out. It puffed and puffed, and rattled along out of the gate and down the lane as fast as ever it could.

As it went it seemed to puff a sort of song, and Malcolm listened to see if he could hear what the words were. It seemed to him as if the engine were singing again and again: 'I *might* be King, yes I *might* be King, I *might* be King, yes I *might* be King!'

'How funny,' said Malcolm. 'Whatever does it mean, Janet? I say, isn't this an adventure!'

The engine tore on down the lane and the two children clung tightly to the sides. At the bottom of the lane they came to a small turning to the right and the engine puffed up this. Janet and Malcolm were astonished.

'I never knew there was a turning here before!' said Janet. 'Did you, Malcolm?'

Malcolm didn't either. But there certainly was, for the engine tore on down the little path, rocking from side to side when stones came in its way. It went on and on and at last came to a steep hill that rose up to a point. The children thought the engine was going to puff right up the hill but it didn't. It ran up to a doorway set deep into the hill and whistled loudly three times.

The door opened at once and the engine ran in, taking the two children with it. As it went in Malcolm heard a noise behind them and he turned round. To his surprise he saw three more engines behind him, one nearly as big as his own, and the others smaller.

They all went down a long passage, chuffing and puffing. At last they came to an enormous cave and there, to the children's great astonishment, they saw hundreds of wooden engines, some painted red, some yellow, some blue and some green. Some were small and some were very big. Malcolm thought his engine must be the biggest of all.

A large red engine whistled for silence, and all the engines stopped chuffing and were still. Then, with a good deal of puffing and blowing, the big engine shouted to the others.

'The King of the Wooden Engines is dead,' he puffed. 'He was broken to pieces yesterday. Who is to be our King now?'

At once all the engines puffed and snorted in excitement, and Malcolm's engine and two other very big ones made their way to the front.

'We are the biggest!' they chuffed. 'One of us must be King!'

Then all the smaller engines rushed round them and whistled excitedly. Malcolm and Janet sat still in the cab of their engine and listened. It was all most exciting. They did hope their engine would be chosen for King!

'This one shall be our King!' puffed the small engines, and they surrounded Malcolm's engine. 'It is the biggest and brightest of all! Where is the paint-pot?'

The big red engine whistled loudly, and a small brownie man rushed in with a pot of bright gold paint. In a flash he had painted a little golden crown round the funnel of Malcolm's engine. Then all the engines whistled at the same time and puffed: 'We greet you, King! Long life to you!'

Malcolm's engine whistled back so loudly that the two children were nearly deafened. Then it put itself at the head of all the engines and began to make its way back to the door in the hillside. Out they all went, the big engine leading the way, puffing and panting a happy little song as it went: 'I'm the King of the Wooden Engines! I'm the King of the Wooden Engines!'

You should have seen the sight as all the brightly painted engines wound their way down the path to the lane. They whistled and puffed merrily. None of them had any children in them except Malcolm's engine, and Malcolm couldn't help thinking how lucky it was that he and Janet had happened to be riding in his engine just when it had rushed off to be made King.

At the end of the path Malcolm's engine turned down the lane that led to their house. The other engines whistled goodbye and went the other way. Malcolm's engine rushed back to the garden and put itself in the very place from where it had started.

'Well!' said Malcolm, as he helped Janet out. 'That *was* an adventure! Fancy, Janet, we've got the King of all the Engines! Aren't we grand?'

They still have that engine. You will know it by the little golden crown painted round the funnel.

Pixie Pins

Lightfoot was a small pixie dressmaker. She was very clever indeed, and she had even made a dress for the Pixie Queen herself. She used spider's thread for her cotton, and rose petals for her material, and she trimmed her gowns and coats with twinkling dewdrops or strips of moonshine. So, you see, it was no wonder all the Little Folk came to her whenever they wanted a new party dress.

One day she had just finished a lovely dress for Princess Peronel. It was made of two yellow rose petals and had a trimming of kingfisher down, so it was very pretty. The kingfisher himself had given Lightfoot the little bits of blue and green down, and he had watched her making the dress.

It was so pretty that he flew all over the place telling everyone about it.

'Lightfoot has made the loveliest gown in the world,' he cried. 'It's the prettiest dress ever I saw!'

Now there was a red goblin who heard him saying this, and he pricked up his big pointed ears. His little wife was always asking him for a new dress, and he wondered if he could steal the new one that Lightfoot had just made. So he followed the kingfisher and asked him some questions.

The kingfisher was only too pleased to tell him all about the new dress.

'Lightfoot has just finished it,' he said. 'She is taking it to the Princess Peronel tonight to fit it on for the last time. It is the loveliest thing ever I saw!'

'Which way is she going to the palace?' asked the goblin slyly.

'Oh, down Cuckoo Lane and past the big horse-chestnut tree!' said the kingfisher, and off he flew, calling out his news about the lovely dress.

The goblin had found out all he wanted to know. That night he hid himself under the hedge in Cuckoo Lane and waited for Lightfoot to come by. Presently he heard her coming, humming a little song. She carried her work-bag with her, and in it she had put the new dress, her measuring tape, her box of pins and some hooks and eyes.

The red goblin pounced out at her with a yell.

She gave a frightened shriek and rushed off down the lane thinking that all the witches and goblins in the world were after her. The red goblin followed her, and poor Lightfoot began to puff and pant. Her work-bag was heavy and she did not dare to drop it, for she didn't want it to be stolen.

She came to the horse-chestnut tree. It stood at the end of the lane, a big tree with umbrella-like leaves. It heard Lightfoot puffing along and called to her.

'Lightfoot! What's the matter? Come, hide inside my trunk if you are frightened! There is a little hole at the bottom where a mouse lives.'

Lightfoot looked for the little hole. She saw a tiny woffly nose looking out of the tree and she guessed it belonged to a mouse. So she ran to it and sure enough, there was the hole in the trunk! She squeezed thankfully into it and heard the red goblin go running past. He didn't know she had hidden in the chestnut tree.

Lightfoot stayed there until all the danger was past. She was very grateful to the tree.

'Can I do anything for you in return for your kindness to me?' she asked.

'No, no; nothing!' answered the tree, and all its leaves whispered: 'No, she can't!'

But the little mouse spoke in Lightfoot's ear. 'There *is* something you can do,' she whispered. 'You know the chestnut grows a lot of fine conkers, and wraps them up in green cases. But the goblins come along and pick them each night before the conkers are ripe, and the tree never has any to throw down for the children. Can you think of a good idea to stop the goblins picking them?'

'Yes, I can!' said Lightfoot, and she took out her box of pins. 'Look, mouse! I'll stick these pins into the conker cases, head downwards, then when the goblins come to pick them they will prick their fingers on the sharp pins, and will soon leave the conkers alone!'

So, after Lightfoot had taken the dress to the Princess, and found that it fitted her beautifully, she flew back to the chestnut tree. She spent the whole night sticking pins head downwards into the green conker cases, and she *did* make them prickly! And when the goblins came slinking along to steal the conkers what a shock they got! They pricked their fingers and scratched their hands terribly, and they howled in surprise and pain.

'It serves you right!' whispered the chestnut leaves in delight. 'It serves you right!'

And ever since then all horse-chestnut conkers have been shut up in very prickly cases to stop the goblins from stealing them. Have you seen them? It's a very good idea, isn't it?

The Adventurous Clown

There was once a clown called Tuffy, who lived in a toyshop with hundreds of other toys. Some of them were very grand toys who wouldn't even look at the little clown, with his painted face and pointed hat. Some were not so grand and the clown would often talk with them.

Tuffy the clown longed to be a hero. He longed to do something grand, something noble so that all the toys in the toyshop would cheer him and cry out that he was a hero. He thought his little corner on a toyshelf was dull. Nothing ever happened there. How could he be a hero when nothing ever happened?

'Why do you grumble so?' asked Timothy, the puppy dog with boot-button eyes and a tail that really wagged. 'Be happy and contented with us, Tuffy. We are a nice little family here on this shelf. Why do you want to go off and have adventures? They might not be nice.'

'Oh, yes, they would be,' said Tuffy.

'Adventures are always exciting. I want to do something really fine. Save someone from a fire or something like that. That would make all the grand toys sit up and take notice. It's so dull up here on our shelf. Why, we only get dusted once a week!'

That night Tuffy the clown climbed down from his shelf. He had made up his mind to seek adventures. There must be lots of them down in the shop. He had heard all sorts of exciting noises at night. Surely grand things must happen down in the shop!

Now that night there was to be a grand race between two wooden horses and carts, driven by wooden farmers. The race was just starting as Tuffy climbed down to the floor. One cart came racing by Tuffy, the farmer standing up and yelling for all he was worth.

Tuffy stood and gaped.

'Goodness! An adventure already!' thought Tuffy. 'A runaway horse! Ha, now is my chance to be a hero!'

The horse and cart came round again, and Tuffy sprang at the reins. He held on to them and dragged the horse to one side. The cart fell over with a crash, and the farmer tipped out. Tuffy stood by, helping him up, feeling very

proud that he had stopped the horse.

But the farmer was terribly angry.

'What do you mean by spoiling my race like that!' he yelled. 'Now the other horse and cart will win! And look at my cart, all on its side! And I've spoilt my best hat, too! You silly, interfering little clown. Take that – and that!'

And the farmer cracked his whip at poor, astonished Tuffy.

'Ooh!' cried Tuffy, rushing away. 'You don't understand! I'm a hero!'

He ran out of sight, and sat down in a toy farm, wiping the tears from his eyes. Horrid man! How dare he crack his whip at him like that when Tuffy had tried to be a hero?

As Tuffy sat there he noticed a doll's house in a corner of the shop – and, dear me, what was that coming out of one of the bedroom windows, in great curls? It was smoke!

'Fire, fire!' yelled Tuffy, jumping to his feet at once. 'Another adventure! Fire! I'll put it out at once!'

He rushed to get a ladder leaning against a haystack. He put it up against the wall of the doll's house. Then he found a big bucket which he filled with water from the farm pond. Up the ladder he went, yelling: 'Fire, fire!'

He threw all the water in at the window, and was just going to climb down for another bucketful, when someone caught him by the collar and roared:

'And what do you think *you're* doing, playing a silly trick like that!'

Poor Tuffy was hauled in through the window and shaken like a rat.

'D-d-don't d-d-do that!' he panted. 'I'm a hero! I was p-p-p-putting out the f-f-f-fire!'

'Fire! What fire?' said the angry voice, and Tuffy saw that he was speaking to a sailor doll who was smoking a large pipe. 'Can't I smoke my pipe without you coming and throwing water all over me? I'll teach you to throw water at people!'

The sailor doll dragged poor Tuffy downstairs and held his head under the cold water tap till he was quite soaked. Then he let him go.

Tuffy staggered out into the shop, shaking the water from his head, and squeezing out his pointed hat.

'They w-w-w-won't let me b-b-b-be a hero,' he sobbed. He walked off, angry and hurt, and sat down on a seat to dry. And as he sat there he heard a cry, and looked round. There was a big globe of water nearby, and in it were swimming two fine goldfish – and in the water was a small doll!

'She's fallen in!' shouted Tuffy, jumping up at once. 'I'll rescue her! This is a real adventure at last!'

He caught hold of a little net which was used to catch the goldfish when they were sold. He clambered up on to a chair and dipped the net into the water. Soon he had caught the little doll and hauled her out – but she slipped out of the net and fell bump on to the table.

She banged her head and began to cry. Up came a policeman doll and said, fiercely: 'What are you doing, catching that doll and making her bump her head like that?'

'I was saving her from drowning!' said Tuffy. 'I am a hero. You ought to cheer me!'

'I was having such a lovely swim!' sobbed the little doll. 'I am a swimming-doll, policeman, and I swim with the goldfish every night. But that horrid clown caught me in a nasty net, and I fell out of it and bumped my head. He isn't a hero. He's just a great, big, interfering NUISANCE!'

'You'd better come along with me,' said the policeman, jerking the clown up with a hard hand. 'Now then – any wriggling and I'll give you a good shaking!'

'I tell you, I'm a hero and –' began the clown, struggling hard. The policeman shook him till all his teeth chattered and his hat fell off. Then off he was marched to prison.

The policeman locked him in a room in the police station and left him there. The clown sat down and put his head in his hands.

'Adventures are horrid,' he groaned, 'Being a hero is silly. If only I were back again on my nice, quiet shelf with Timothy Dog and the others.'

Suddenly he heard a little noise outside the window of the room. 'Tuffy! Tuffy!' barked a little voice. 'It is I, Timothy. Here is the key to the door, coming in at the window!'

Tinkle! The key fell to the floor and the clown quickly undid the door. He and Timothy ran off together and climbed up to the shelf. Tuffy hugged the kind little dog and thanked him very much.

'*You're* the hero!' he said. 'All the things I did were silly, not wonderful or noble. I didn't stop to think. But you saw I was in real trouble and saved me.'

'Don't mention it,' said the toy dog, blushing. 'I don't want to be a hero, I'm sure.'

'Oh, how lovely and peaceful it is up on this shelf,' said Tuffy, looking round happily. 'I never want to leave it again.'

And, until he was sold, he never did!

The Money That Flew Away

Malcolm and Jessie were most excited because Mummy was going to take them to the Fair that afternoon. They had all saved up, and Mummy had a ten-pound note in her purse to take them. That would pay for their tickets, their tea, some coconut shies and some roundabouts. What fun they would have!

That morning Mummy opened her purse to take out some money to pay the baker – and, oh dear me, what a dreadful thing, the ten-pound note fell out and was blown away by the wind!

'Quick, quick, go after it, children!' cried Mummy. They ran out into the garden, and chased the flying note, which was being blown away fast by the wind. Suddenly Malcolm and Jessie lost sight of it. They hunted here and they hunted there – but it was gone. Wherever could it have flown to?

The children hunted for more than half an hour, but they couldn't find the ten-pound note.

They were very unhappy. Suppose Mummy said they couldn't go to the Fair now?

That's just what she *did* say! 'I'm very sorry, dears,' she said, 'but I really can't afford to take you if we've lost that ten pounds. Isn't it a shame?'

Mummy looked so miserable that Malcolm and Jessie flung their arms round her and kissed her.

'Never mind, Mummy!' they cried. 'We won't make a fuss! Perhaps it will turn up some other day and we can buy something nice with it.'

It was kind of them to be so good about it, wasn't it? Mummy was very pleased.

'Would you like to take a broom each and go to sweep up the dead leaves in the garden?' she said. 'I know you like doing that. You can make a bonfire of them if you like.'

'Yes, we'd love that!' cried Jessie, and off they went with a broom each. They were pleased to think they could help to tidy up the garden for their mother. They swept up the leaves into a big heap, and then ran indoors for some matches.

Jessie lit the dry leaves and they flared up – and just as the bonfire was burning up merrily,

Malcolm gave a loud shout.

'Jessie! There's the ten-pound note, all among the leaves! Quick, give me that stick and I'll try to rake it out before it's burnt!'

He just managed to poke it out before the flames caught it – and then, shouting in excitement the children rushed indoors to their mother.

'Mummy, Mummy, we've found the ten-pound note! It had blown among the dead leaves, and that was why we couldn't find it. Can we go to the Fair now?'

'Of course!' said Mummy, delighted. 'I *am* glad! Just think, children, if you hadn't been so good and helpful, you would never have found the money. Well, you really do deserve your treat!'

When the Toys Walked Home

Sheila had a lovely dolls' pram and she took her dolls and her teddy-bear out in it every day for a nice long walk. She never missed a day, and all the toys enjoyed their walk very much.

One day the little girl next door asked Sheila if she would lend her pram just for that morning.

'Oh, do, Sheila,' she begged. 'I have never had a pram, and I would so like to wheel one just once. Do lend me yours.'

'But my dolls will miss their walk dreadfully if I let you have my pram this morning,' said Sheila. 'Besides, you might break it, or run into something on the pavement.'

'I wouldn't,' said Ann, the little girl. 'I would be very careful, I wouldn't take your pram out on the road, Sheila. I would just wheel it round and round my garden.'

'My dolls will be so disappointed if I don't take them for their ride,' said Sheila, looking at them as they all sat ready in the dolls' pram.

'Well, can't you take them for a walk instead?' asked Ann. 'You could take their hands, couldn't you, and let them walk with you for once, instead of riding in their pram.'

'Don't be silly!' said Sheila. 'Toys can't really walk. You know that! I only wish they could. I'd love to see them walking down the road just like you and me. It would be lovely. Well, Ann, I *will* lend you my pram just for this morning, if you'll be careful with it. And I will take my toys in the wheelbarrow just for once. It will be a change for them.'

So Ann wheeled the pram into her own garden and put *her* dolls into it. And Sheila fetched her little wheelbarrow and sat her three dolls and her brown teddy-bear in it. It was rather a squash but they didn't seem to mind.

Off she went to the woods. She thought it would be nice and shady there, and there might be blackberries ripening. It would be nice to pick some.

There *were* some blackberries! Sheila began to pick some from a big bush – and then she suddenly saw the funniest little man she had ever seen, picking blackberries from the *other* side of the bush! As she watched him, she heard him say to himself, 'Bother! Oh, bother, bother! Here's my basket gone and got an enormous hole in it just when I wanted to take home enough blackberries to make some pots of blackberry jam!'

Sheila peeped over the bush at his basket. It certainly had a very big hole in it and the blackberries were dropping out as fast as he put them in. He really looked ready to cry!

Then he saw Sheila and he stared at her in surprise. 'Hello, little girl!' he said. 'Just look at my basket! Isn't it too bad! Now I shan't be able to take any blackberries home to make into jam, and my wife will be *so* cross with me.'

'I'm very sorry,' said Sheila, politely. 'I haven't brought a basket with me or I would have lent you one. I'm just taking my toys for a walk in my wheelbarrow.'

'Wheelbarrow!' said the little man excitedly, running round the bush to see it. 'Just the thing! *Just* the thing! Will you lend it to me to carry home my blackberries, little girl? I could put heaps of them into that nice big barrow, and my wife would be so pleased.'

'But what about my dolls?' said Sheila. 'I can't carry them all home, you know!'

'Why can't they walk?' asked the little man, at once.

'Don't be silly!' said Sheila, quite cross at having the same question asked her twice in one morning. 'You know toys can't walk. I only wish they could! If they could, I'd lend you my barrow at once!'

'Will you!' cried the little man, in delight. 'Well, I can easily make your toys walk. Dolls and teddy-bear, get out of the barrow and walk home with the little girl!'

And then, to Sheila's great astonishment, the three dolls and the teddy-bear all climbed quickly out of the barrow and ran up to her, holding up hands and paws for her to take. She stared at them in surprise and delight.

'Well, look at that!' she said at last. 'They have all come alive and will walk home with me. Whatever will people say!'

The little man ran to the empty barrow and wheeled it to his side of the bush. Then he began very quickly to pick blackberries and throw them into the barrow.

'I'll bring your barrow back tomorrow,' he called. 'Thank you so much, little girl. Goodbye!'

The toys dragged at Sheila's hands, and she turned to go home again. She called goodbye to the busy little man and then took the hands of her two smallest dolls, who in their turn took hands with the third doll and the bear. Then all five walked homewards through the wood. You should have seen how delighted Sheila was! The toys walked very nicely indeed, and laughed for joy at having such a treat.

Sheila met two or three people on the way home and you should have seen how they stared! Sheila felt so proud to be taking out a toy family. As she passed Ann's gate, Ann came runnning up – and how *she* stared to see Sheila and the toys all walking home together!

Sheila told her what had happened, and Ann was delighted.

'It's a reward for you because you were so kind and lent me your dolls' pram!' she said. 'But look, Sheila, the littlest doll is looking so tired. Here is your pram – let's put the toys in it, for they are not used to such a long walk.'

So into the pram they were all packed, and Sheila wheeled them into her own garden. She felt so excited and pleased to think that her toys had walked home with her. She was sure that such a thing had never happened to any other little girl.

In the morning she found her wheelbarrow in the garden, left there by the little man. And what do you think was inside it? Why, a little tiny pot of blackberry jam, put there for Sheila, in return for her kindness in lending her wheel-barrow. Isn't she lucky?

Twelve Little Pigs

Once upon a time a dozen little pigs ran into Miss Trippy's garden. She saw them from her bedroom window and she tapped on the pane, crying: 'Little pigs, little pigs, go out at once!'

But they took no notice of her at all.

Then she sent for her dog, Rover, and told him to go and chase the pigs away. He went and barked at them, but they were having such a good time, nibbling the lettuces and gobbling the peas that they took no notice of him either.

'Wuff, wuff!' he barked. 'Go out at once, little pigs!'

But they stayed among the peas and didn't even turn to look at him. Then Miss Trippy sent for her cat, and told her to go and chase the pigs away.

So Cinders the cat ran out, snarling and hissing.

'Little pigs, little pigs, go out at once!' she mewed. 'Miaow! S-ss-ss!'

But the little pigs took no notice of Cinders at all. They had found some carrots and were rooting them up in delight. Poor Miss Trippy! She wondered whatever she could do.

Then she sent for Captain, the big carthorse that belonged to the farmer, and told him to gallop up to the pigs and chase them away.

So he came trotting up to the garden gate, and galloped up the path to the kitchen garden. Cloppity-cloppity-clop, his hoofs went, and he neighed loudly. Ha! *He* would frighten away those wicked little pigs!

'Pooh! It's only a horse,' grunted the pigs, and they took no notice of him at all. They were used to horses. There were five at the farm where they had come from.

The big horse neighed again, and galloped about after the pigs – but soon Miss Trippy knocked loudly at the window, because he was doing a great deal of damage with his big hoofs.

So he cantered out of the gate, and left the little pigs still enjoying themselves among the peas and carrots.

Then a boy came by with a big stick. Miss Trippy called to him and begged him to drive away the little pigs with his stick. So in at the gate he went, shouting and halloing for all he was worth.

'Shoo, shoo, shoo!' he yelled. 'Get away, you wicked little pigs! Shoo, shoo, shoo!'

The pigs scattered here and there, but as fast as he drove one away another ran back, and it wasn't a bit of use. They took no notice of him at all!

Miss Trippy didn't know *what* to do! But just then a small wasp, striped in yellow and black, came buzzing by.

'Zzzzzzzz!' it said. 'Dogs, cats, horses, boys – none of them can chase out pigs! Zzzzzz! But I can though I am only small. Let me come and steal a few of your sweet apples in the autumn, Miss Trippy, and I will chase away the pigs for you.'

'Very well,' said Miss Trippy. 'But it is hardly likely that a little thing like you will be able to do what even a great horse cannot do! You think too much of yourself, wasp!'

'A little thing is sometimes better than a big thing!' buzzed the wasp, and off it went into the garden. 'Zzzzzz!' it buzzed to the pigs. 'Go away at once! Zzzzzz!'

The pigs took no notice, but went on rooting up carrots. The wasp flew to one and stung it on the nose. It squealed with pain and rushed straight out of the gate!' Zzzzzz!' went the wasp. 'Zzzzzz!' Another little pig was stung on the nose and then a third one on its curly tail. The garden was soon full of grunts and squeals, and one by one the little pigs rushed out of the gate. Miss Trippy ran out into the garden and banged the gate shut. The pigs were out at last!

'What did I tell you?' buzzed the wasp, sailing round her head. 'Will you let me have an apple or two when they are ripe?'

'Willingly!' cried Miss Trippy. 'You were quite right, wasp! A little thing is sometimes better than a big thing! Help yourself to as many apples and pears as you wish!'

It did! Not only that but it brought all its relations, too, and *what* a feast they had!

The Little Pop-gun

The day that Willie bought his pop-gun was a dreadful one for all the rest of the toys in his nursery. They had never heard of any sort of gun before, and none of them knew what a pop-gun was.

Willie brought his gun proudly into the nursery. Then he stood up his wooden soldiers in a row, and put the cork into the end of his pop-gun. It was tied on to the gun by a string. When Willie pressed the trigger of the gun the cork flew out with a loud pop and hit one of the wooden soldiers. He fell over at once. Then Willie put back the cork in the gun and shot it out at the next soldier.

Pop! He went over too!

'What a fine pop-gun I have!' cried Willie. 'Now I will shoot all my skittles over!'

So he stood up his big skittles and one by one he shot those over too. Then his mother called him to dinner, and he went, leaving his pop-gun on the floor. As soon as Willie was out of the room all the soldiers and skittles picked themselves up and scuttled back to the toy-cupboard as fast as ever they could go. They were very much afraid of the pop-gun! The teddy-bear and two dolls hid themselves at the back of the cupboard, too.

'What a dreadful new toy that is, that Willie has brought to our nursery!' said the teddy-bear in a whisper. 'It shouts "POP" at us and then knocks us over. I can't bear it!'

'Hi, where are you all going to?' suddenly shouted the pop-gun from its place in the middle of the floor. 'Come and be friendly. Talk to me and tell me all about this nursery I've come to live in.'

'We don't like you,' said the soldiers, all together. 'You shout "POP" at the top of your voice and then you punch us in the middle and knock us down.'

'Pooh!' said the pop-gun, laughing. 'I won't really hurt you, toys. A pop-gun always says "pop" when the trigger is pulled. As for knocking you down, don't mind that. It is only my little cork that knocks you over – it doesn't really hurt you. It's just a game.'

But none of the toys would make friends with

the pop-gun or go near him. He had to stay by himself all day and all night, for, wherever he was, the toys left him alone, and if he tried to talk to them they wouldn't listen. They thought he was a horrid, rough, unkind toy. But he couldn't help being a pop-gun, and he was sad because the toys wouldn't be friends.

Willie had a pet, beside all his toys. This was Whiskers, his little black cat. She slept in the nursery very often and the toys were quite fond of her. She had a little round basket near the fire.

One day Willie looked into Whiskers' basket and gave a shout of surprise.

'Mummy! Whiskers has got four little black kittens in her basket. Oh, how lovely!'

It was quite true. The toys peeped to see, and sure enough they spied four tiny black creatures cuddled up against Whiskers, who was very pleased.

But, you know, when those kittens grew big enough to climb out of their basket, how they teased the poor toys! They were wild, mischievous little creatures, and they used to climb into the toy-cupboard after the toys, and dig their sharp little claws into them till they squealed! They tore the dolls' pretty dresses with their sharp teeth, and they licked all the sweets in the toy sweet-shop. The toys became frightened of the four kittens.

The teddy-bear went to Whiskers one night and spoke to her.

'Whiskers,' he said, 'the toys have asked me to beg you to take your little kittens away somewhere else. They are unkind to us and we don't want them to live in the nursery.'

Whiskers hissed at the teddy-bear in a rage. 'How dare you say my kittens are unkind!' she cried. 'I shall certainly not take them away. They are the dearest, sweetest kittens in the world, and if they want to tease you, they can. You should stand up for yourselves. They are only kittens.'

The kittens grew bigger and bigger, and, dear me, the poor toys were more and more afraid of them. The pop-gun used to watch the kittens scratching and biting – and then, when he saw the very prettiest doll having her hair pulled off her little head, he made up his mind to rescue the toys. They hadn't been kind to him, but never mind!

He called to the teddy-bear.

'Hi, Teddy! I'll help you to get rid of those mischievous little kittens! Come and pick me up and put my cork in. Press the trigger and make my cork jump out at the kittens. They will soon stop teasing you!'

Teddy ran across the floor and picked up the little pop-gun. He pressed the cork in at the end of the gun and then pointed at the nearest kitten, who was running at him to scratch him.

'Pop!' The cork sprang out of the pop-gun half an inch from the kitten's nose. It darted back in fright. The other kittens came round the teddy-bear, spitting and hissing. Teddy quickly fitted in the cork again.

'Pop!' The cork sprang out to the full length of his string, and if the nearest kitten hadn't sprung backwards, the cork would have hit its front paw.

'S-S-sssssssss!' spat all the kittens. Whiskers heard them hissing and jumped out of her basket. She ran at Teddy in a rage, her paw raised to cuff him.

'Pop!' The cork made her stop in fright.

'Mew! Whatever is it?' she cried. 'Come, kittens, this is dangerous. Follow me, and we will go away from this horrible pop-thing. It might eat us up!'

She ran out of the nursery with all her four kittens following her. She took them to the kitchen, where the dog had a basket, and told them all to sleep there. She wasn't going back to the nursery again!

'There!' said the pop-gun, pleased. 'What did I tell you? They've gone and they won't come back. You'll have a little peace now, Teddy, you and the rest of the toys. Go and tell them.'

Teddy put the pop-gun down on the floor and ran to tell the toys. In a moment they all swarmed out of the toy-cupboard and ran to the pop-gun. They picked him up and put him on their shoulders. Then they carried him round the nursery, shouting: 'For he's a jolly good fellow! For he's a jolly good fellow!' till they were quite out of breath.

'We're sorry we thought you were a rough, unkind creature!' they said. 'You have done us a very good turn. Thank you.'

'Well, now perhaps you'll be friends with me,' said the pop-gun, making his cork jump up and down in the air.

'Of course!' cried everyone, and they took him straight back to the toy-cupboard to sleep with them. And ever since then the pop-gun has had so many friends that he has really never been able to count them!

Quizzy the Goblin

Quizzy was a small green goblin who was always poking his long nose into everything. He really was a perfect nuisance. He wanted to know this and he wanted to know that. He always longed to know every secret there was, and if people wouldn't tell him he flew into a rage and blew green flames out of his mouth.

So nobody liked him very much, and most people were afraid of him. He lived in a hole in the middle of an apple tree that tapped against a nursery window. He often ran up the tree and, if the window was open, hopped into the nursery.

Then the toys would sigh and say: 'Oh bother! Here's Quizzy again. Now we shan't have any peace at all!'

Quizzy wanted to know everything. He wanted to know how to wind up the clockwork engine, and how to set the clockwork mouse going. As soon as he knew he set the engine and mouse going, and they bumped straight into one another. The mouse hurt his nose, and the engine had a bump on its front. They were very cross.

But Quizzy laughed till the tears ran down his cheeks. That was the sort of thing he thought was really funny.

Then another time he wanted to know how the musical box worked, and he wound the handle round so often that it became worn out and broke. The toys were very angry about that, for they loved the tinkling music that came out of the musical box. The clockwork clown scolded the goblin for breaking it, and he flew into a rage at once.

Green flames shot out of his mouth and burnt a hole in the nursery carpet. The toys were frightened and rushed to the toy-cupboard. They climbed in and shut the door – but that wicked little goblin blew a green flame through the key-hole and burnt a hole in the big doll's dress. She screamed, and the goblin laughed loudly.

'That will teach you to interfere with me!' he cried. 'I shall do exactly as I like in your nursery, so there!'

With that he jumped out of the window and disappeared down the apple tree. The toys were so glad to see him go.

'If only we could give him a real fright so that he would never come back again!' sighed the big doll, trying to mend the hole in her pretty blue dress.

'But we can't!' said the clockwork clown. 'Because, for one thing, he would never go near anything he was afraid of – and for another thing I don't believe there *is* anything he is frightened of!'

Now the very next day what should come to the nursery but a large red box in which was hidden a jack-in-the-box with a very long spring to make him jump right out as soon as the lid was opened.

The toys all knew what a jack-in-the-box was, for there had been plenty in the toyshops where they came from – but they wondered if the goblin knew. Perhaps he didn't! If he didn't, what a fright he would get if only they could make him open the box! But how could they make him? If they told him to he would certainly think there was some trick about it, and wouldn't go near it!

'I know!' said the clockwork clown, who was always the one to get good ideas. 'I know! Let's pretend to hide the box away, and beg the goblin not to touch it. Then he is sure to wonder what it is, and he is such a one for poking his nose everywhere that he is certain to lift up the lid sooner or later – then whooooosh! The jack-in-the-box will jump out, and *what* a fright he'll get!'

The big doll wrote out a notice and put it against the box. The notice said: '*Do not touch*!'

'That will make the goblin want to touch it as soon as he sees it!' said the doll, with a laugh.

The next time the goblin came in at the window the toys caught hold of the box and pretended that they were trying to hide it away from Quizzy. He saw them at once and ran up.

'What's that you're trying to hide away?' he cried. 'Is it a secret?'

'Yes, it is, and *you're* not to find out our secret!' cried the teddy-bear.

'What's in the box?' shouted Quizzy, excitedly.

'Never you mind!' said the clockwork clown.

'Is it gold?' asked Quizzy. 'Or something nice to eat? Or fine new clothes?'

'It doesn't matter what it is, you're not to look and see!' said all the toys together.

Well, of course, that made Quizzy more determined than ever that he *would* peep inside that box and see what there was in it. How dare the toys have a secret he didn't know.

He didn't quite like to make the toys show him the inside of the box, when they were all so determined not to, so he made up his mind to come back just before cock-crow, when the toys would have climbed into the toy-cupboard to sleep. Then he would open the box and find out the great secret! And if it was gold he would take it for himself. If it was something nice to eat, he would eat it – and if it was fine clothes he would wear them. Ha ha! That would teach the toys to keep their secrets from Quizzy the goblin!

He jumped out of the window. The toys smiled at one another. They knew quite well he would come back at cock-crow!

They were all in the toy-cupboard, peeping, when Quizzy did come back. He tiptoed across the nursery floor to where the box stood with its notice leaning against it: '*Do not touch!*'

The goblin tore the notice in half. Then he looked at the lid of the box. How was it opened? Ah! There was a little catch. If he slipped that back he could open the lid.

He pressed it back. The lid flew off with a bang, and whoooooooosh! Out leapt the jack-in-the-box, squeaking with all his might, his red face shining, his black hair standing up on end! He knocked the goblin flat on his face, and then

hung over him, wobbling about on his long spring, a really fearsome sight!

The goblin got up and gave one look at him. Then he yelled with fright and tore to the window as fast as he could run.

'A witch, a witch!' he cried, and jumped right out of the window. Down the apple tree he slid and landed bump on the ground. Then he began to run. He ran, and ran, and ran – and, so the toys say, he is *still* running! Anyway, he has never come back, and you should see the jack-in-the-box laugh when he tells the tale of how he frightened Quizzy the goblin. You'd love to watch him!

The Kind Hedgehog

When John and Sallie went out in the garden one morning, they ran to watch their father taking down the tennis net. Summer was over and autumn was in, making the mornings crisp and cool.

'Can we help to take down the nets all round the court?' asked Sallie. 'We'd like to.'

'Yes,' said their father. 'Unhook them from the posts and roll them up neatly.'

So the children began. Soon they came to a net that seemed to have a great knot at the bottom of it. They shook it but the knot stayed. It was heavy.

'It can't be a knot!' cried John. 'It's something else. Daddy, what's this?' Daddy came over.

'Why, it's a poor little hedgehog that has walked into the net at the bottom and got tangled up in it,' he said. 'I'll have to cut the net to get him out.'

'The naughty little thing!' cried Sallie, as she watched Daddy cut the net. 'The net was new this summer – now the hedgehog has spoilt it. There will be a big hole there next summer for balls to roll through.'

'It's a nasty, tiresome little hedgehog,' said John. 'It ought to be punished.'

Just then Mother came up to see what all the excitement was about. She looked down at the little rolled-up hedgehog that Daddy had cut out of the net.

'Poor little thing,' she said. 'So you came wandering across the grass looking for beetles and grubs, and got caught in the net. How frightened you must have been! And there was nobody to help you or cut you loose till the children found you this morning. I am sorry for you, little hedgehog. I hope you are not dead with fright.'

Mother picked up the hedgehog carefully. It was very prickly indeed, but she knew just how to hold it so that the spines did not prick her.

'We will give it some cat food,' she said. 'It will like that. Come along and help me, children.'

John and Sallie no longer wanted to punish the little hedgehog. They wanted to help it instead. Off they all went, and very soon they had the delight of seeing the funny little brown creature uncurl itself and run to the saucer of cat food. It ate it all with its funny little snout-like mouth, and looked at them with bright, beady eyes.

'Now we will let it run off,' said Mother. The hedgehog must have heard what she said, for it ran to the bushes and soon disappeared.

'Let's leave some cat food out for it tonight,' said Sallie. 'It might come back.'

'I wish it would do a good deed in return for our kindness,' said Mother. 'You know, our kitchen is simply full of horrid black beetles at night. I can't get rid of them. They come out from under the stove and walk all over the place. I wish the hedgehog would eat them for me.'

'Let's leave the cat food by the kitchen door,' said Sallie. 'We could leave the door open a little way, and if it's a nice kind hedgehog it will come in and eat our beetles, Isn't that a good idea, Mummy?'

So that night the two children put down a saucer of cat food by the back door, and left the door just a little bit open – enough for a little hedgehog to creep through if it wanted to.

Next morning the cat food was still there.

Sallie and John wondered if the hedgehog had seen it, but had made up its mind to eat the beetles instead.

'Let's creep downstairs and see tonight,' said Sallie. So that night, when everyone was asleep in bed, and the clock had struck twelve, the two children crept downstairs to the kitchen. They hated to go to the kitchen late at night, because of the beetles there, but they did so badly want to see if the hedgehog had come back.

He had! Well, you should have seen him! He was scurrying about the floor, gobbling up the nasty black beetles as fast as ever he could! They came out from the nooks and crannies under the warm stove, where they had lived for years, and as soon as the hedgehog saw them he ran over to them. His sharp little teeth snapped them up, and that was the end of the beetles!

'Just look!' whispered Sallie. 'That little hedgehog is getting rid of all those horrid beetles that spoil our kitchen! Beetles that live in kitchens have to be destroyed, Mummy says, but she has never been able to send them off before! Now the hedgehog is doing it for us!'

As soon as the hedgehog heard their voices he ran straight out of the kitchen door in fright. The children stayed quite quiet – and soon they saw his sharp little snout peeping in again. 'Is everything quiet?' he seemed to say. 'Then I will get back to my supper!'

Back he came, and soon the black beetles hurried away to their holes in fear. The children went back to bed longing to tell their mother all they had seen.

'We know why the hedgehog doesn't eat his cat food!' said Sallie to their mother next morning. 'It's because he's doing you a good turn, Mummy, and eating all your black beetles for you!'

'The kind little fellow!' said Mother. 'I did hope he would. We will leave a little cat food out each night for him, and as soon as he begins to eat it we shall know he has cleared out all those beetles for us!'

That little hedgehog came back to the kitchen every single night, and in a week's time, when Sallie was sitting in the kitchen, there was not a single beetle to be seen.

'Well, Mummy,' she said, 'all those creepy-crawly beetles have gone. I hope they don't come back.'

'They won't come back, Sallie!' said Mother. 'The hedgehog has eaten them all! Hasn't he been a good friend to us!'

'Well,' said Sallie. 'The hedgehog we got out of the tennis net must have said to itself: "One good turn deserves another!" and that's why it ate your beetles!'

'I shouldn't be surprised,' said Mother. 'It's always best to be kind to everything, big or little, smooth or prickly. You never know when you might need their help!'

The Cold Snowman

It happened once that some children built a great big snowman. You should have seen him! He was as tall as you, but much fatter, and he wore an old top hat, so he looked very grand. On his hands were woollen gloves, but they were rather holey. Down his front were large round pebbles for buttons and round his neck was an old woollen scarf. He really looked very grand indeed.

The children went indoors at tea-time, and didn't come out again, because it was dark. So the snowman stood all alone in the back yard, and he was very lonely.

He began to sigh, and Foolish-One, the little elf who lived under the old apple tree, heard him and felt sorry. He ran out and spoke to the snowman.

'Are you lonely?' he asked.

'Very,' answered the snowman.

'Are you cold?' asked Foolish-One.

'Who wouldn't be in this frosty weather?' said the snowman.

'I'm sorry for you,' said Foolish-One. 'Shall I sing to you?'

'If you like,' said the snowman. So the elf began to sing a doleful little song about a star that fell from the sky and couldn't get back. It was so sad that the snowman cried a few tears, and they froze at once on his white, snowy cheeks.

'Stop singing that song,' he begged the elf. 'It makes me cry, and it is very painful to do that when your tears freeze on you. Ooooh! Isn't the wind cold?'

'Poor snowman!' said Foolish-One, tying the snowman's scarf so tightly that he nearly choked.

'Don't do that!' gasped the snowman. 'You're strangling me.'

'You have no coat,' said Foolish-One, looking sadly at the snowman. 'You will be frozen stiff before morning.'

'Oooh!' said the snowman, in alarm. 'Frozen stiff! That sounds dreadful! I wish I wasn't so cold.'

'Shall I get you a nice warm coat?' asked the elf. 'I have one that would keep you very cosy.'

'Well, seeing that you only come up to my knees, I'm afraid that your coat would only be big enough for a handkerchief for me,' said the snowman. 'Ooh! There's that cold wind again.'

Just then a smell of burning came over the air, and the elf sniffed it. He jumped to his feet in excitement. Just the thing!

'Snowman!' he cried. 'There's a bonfire. I can smell it. Let us go to it and warm ourselves.'

The snowman tried to move. He was very heavy, and little bits of snow broke off him. But at last he managed to shuffle along somehow, and he followed the dancing elf down the garden path to the corner of the garden where the bonfire was burning.

'Here we are!' said the elf, in delight. 'See what a fine blaze there is. Come, snowman, draw close, and I will tell you a story.'

The snowman came as close to the fire as he could. It was certainly very warm. He couldn't feel the cold wind at all now. It was much better.

'Once upon a time,' began the elf, 'there was a princess called Marigold. Are you nice and warm, snowman?'

'Very,' said the snowman, drowsily. The heat was making him sleepy. 'Go on, Foolish-One.'

'Now this princess lived in a high castle,' went on Foolish-One, leaning against the snowman as he talked. 'And one day – are you sure you're quite warm, snowman?'

'Very, very warm,' murmured the snowman, his hat slipping to one side of his head. Plonk! One of his stone buttons fell off. Plonk! Then another. How odd!

Foolish-One went on with his story. It wasn't a very exciting one, and the snowman hardly listened. He was so warm and sleepy. Foolish-One suddenly felt sleepy, too. He stopped in the middle of his tale and shut his eyes. Then very gently he began to snore.

He woke up with a dreadful jump, for he heard a most peculiar noise.

'Sizzle-sizzle-sizzle, ss-ss-sss-ss!'

Whatever could it be? He jumped up. The fire was almost out. The snowman had gone! Only his hat, scarf and gloves remained, and they were in a pile on the ground.

'Who has put the fire out?' cried Foolish-One in a rage. 'Snowman, where are you? Why have you gone off and left all your clothes? You will catch your death of cold!'

But the snowman didn't answer. He was certainly quite gone. Foolish-One began to cry.

The fire was quite out now, and a pool of water lay all round it. Who had poured the water there? And where, oh where, was that nice snowman?

He called him up the garden and down. He hunted for him everywhere. Then he went home and found his thickest coat and warmest hat. He put them on, took his stick and went out.

'I will find that snowman if it takes me a thousand years to do it!' he cried. And off he went to begin his search. He hasn't found him yet! Poor Foolish-One, I don't somehow think he ever will!

The Big Green Handkerchief

Twinkle the elf had a big green handkerchief that he was very fond of. He always put it into his pocket on Saturday, which was market day, for then he could pull it out and show it to a lot of people.

One Saturday he put it into his pocket as usual and went off to market. When he got there he went round looking at all the cows and sheep, and he bought himself three new-laid eggs and a pound of yellow butter.

Just as he was turning a corner he fell over a duck that was wandering about by itself. Bang! Over went Twinkle and hit his head on the pavement. Everyone ran to pick him up and made a fuss of him.

'He's cut his head,' said kind Mother Dimple. 'We must bandage it up.'

A little bit of the green handkerchief was sticking out of Twinkle's pocket, so Mother Dimple pulled it out and bandaged Twinkle's head with it. He didn't notice what she was doing for he really felt quite bad. But soon he felt better, especially when someone brought him a nice hot sausage roll to eat.

He got up, dusted his trousers and said thank you. Then off he went. He hadn't gone very far before he met Mr Whiskers, who had a very fine red handkerchief in his pocket, which he showed to Twinkle.

'See what I had for my birthday,' he said. Then Twinkle put his hand in his pocket to show Mr Whiskers his fine green handkerchief – and it wasn't there! Dear, dear! He turned out all his pockets one after another, but it wasn't in any of them. Whatever could have happened to it? Someone must have stolen it out of his pocket!

He rushed off to see if he could find it. He saw something green in the distance and he ran after it. It was sticking out from underneath Dame Penny's arm. *She* must have taken his handkerchief! Twinkle tugged at it – and oh, my goodness me, it wasn't a handkerchief after all, but a green sunshade!

Dame Penny was angry! She shook her sunshade at Twinkle and said she would spank him with it. He rushed off in a great hurry.

Then he saw something green going round the corner. That must be his handkerchief. Off he raced and turned the corner. The muffin-man was going down the street and on his head was a tray covered by something green.

'That's my handkerchief!' thought Twinkle, and he rushed up to the muffin-man. He tore the covering from the tray – but, oh dear, dear, dear, it was the green cloth that the muffin-man always used to cover up his muffins! He *was* cross with Twinkle!

'I'll smack you if I catch you!' he cried. But Twinkle was off!

Then he saw something green hanging out on Mother Crotchety's line – it must be his handkerchief! He crept into the garden and tore the green thing off the line – but Mother Crotchety was there and she boxed his ears.

'What do you mean by taking my nice green duster!' she shouted. 'You naughty little elf!'

Twinkle ran out of the gate. This was dreadful. Wherever in the world could his handkerchief be?

'It's no good,' he said. 'I must go home. I shall never find it.'

So he went down the street to his cottage, feeling very sad indeed.

'I shall never see my handkerchief again,' he sighed.

When he reached home his little wife cried out in surprise to see him with his head bound up.

'Oh, I just fell down and hurt myself,' said Twinkle.

'Well, let me bathe the place,' said his little wife, and she carefully undid the bandage. She placed it on the table and Twinkle saw it. He stared and stared and stared.

'Ooh, my!' he said, in astonishment. 'There's my handkerchief. Was it on my head all the time, little wife?'

'Of course,' said his wife surprised. 'Why?'

'Because I've been rushing about all over the place taking things I thought were my green handkerchief, and all the time it was round my head,' groaned Twinkle. 'What a silly I am!'

He was a bit of a silly, wasn't he!

The Golden Peacock

Once upon a time, many thousands of years ago when the world was very young, a cobbler going on his rounds found something glittering in the dusty road. He picked it up, and found, to his surprise, that it was a golden peacock.

It was small, and most beautifully made. It had rubies for eyes, and in its outspread tail were set many tiny jewels. It was a lovely thing.

The cobbler was an honest man and he took his find to the King.

'Ah!' said the King, turning it over and over in his hand. 'This is a treasure beyond price. See how beautifully wrought this peacock is! How many weeks, how many months have gone to the setting of these tiny jewels in the fine, outspread tail! I should like to buy this golden peacock and set it on my marble shelf where all may see it. I will send a messenger through the land proclaiming the find, asking the maker of the peacock to come forward.'

The messenger was sent out – and the next week, to the King's surprise, two men came to claim the peacock!

'What?' cried the King. 'You both own the golden peacock? That is impossible. One of you is speaking falsely.'

The two men glared at one another. One was called Moola, and the other Gron. Both were workers in silver and gold, and each vowed that he had made the golden peacock himself, and lost it on a journey.

The King looked at them sternly.

'One of you does not speak the truth,' he said. 'It would be easy for me to send to your towns, and ask your friends which of you has made the peacock, for such a marvellous piece of work is sure to be well-known.'

'Sire,' said Moola, at once, 'it would be of no use sending to my town, for no one knows of this peacock. I did it in secret, for my own pleasure, and no one has seen the lovely bird. I was keeping it to take to the great market in the autumn.'

'So!' said the King, mockingly. 'It was a secret! And you, Gron, what do you say? Was the peacock also a secret with you? Will those in your town know of this golden bird?'

'Sire,' said Gron, his hands trembling as he spoke, 'none but myself knows of the bird. I made it in secret, and these words are the truth.'

The King laughed in scorn. 'I believe you both speak falsely,' he said. 'Tell me, Gron, why should you fashion such a marvellous thing in secret? Have you a reason like Moola's?'

'I have a reason,' said Gron, 'but it is not like Moola's. I made the golden bird for my little daughter's birthday. It was to be a surprise, and none knew of it save myself. I spent all my nights on the bird, Sire, and each of those little jewels took me a whole week to set to my liking.'

'False fellow!' shouted Moola, the other goldsmith. '*I* set those tiny jewels in the tail! Many, many days did I work on those finely-wrought feathers, and the beak I modelled no less than eleven times before it was perfect!'

'Silence,' said the King sternly. 'Now this is a puzzle harder than any I had to solve before. So lovely is this bird that I had resolved to buy it from its rightful owner – but it seems that both of you are the owners, though how that can be is beyond my understanding.'

'It is mine!' said Moola, sulkily.

'Nay, it is mine!' cried Gron, falling on his knees.

'Give it to me, o King, and I will sell it to you for half the price you meant to give!' said Moola. The King turned to Gron.

'And you?' he asked. 'Would you also sell it to me for half the price I had meant to give, if I award the bird to you, Gron?'

Gron was silent.

'Answer me,' commanded the King.

'Sire,' said Gron, stammering in his nervousness, 'as I told you, it was meant for my little daughter. I would rather give it to her for whom it was meant.'

The King looked at both the men for a long moment. Then he spoke.

'Seeing that both of you say you own the bird,' he said, at last, 'and I have no means of finding out which of you speaks the truth, I can do no better than to order the bird to be cut in half. Then one of you shall have the head and the other the tail. For that you must draw lots.'

'Agreed, o King,' said Moola, at once. Gron was silent.

'And you, Gron, do you agree?' asked the King, looking at the pale goldsmith.

Gron threw himself down before the King.

'Do not cut the bird in half, Sire!' he cried. 'It is so beautiful! I spent so much labour on it! It would spoil it to be halved. What is the use of a head or tail? The bird is not just gold and jewels, it is a piece of loveliness. I would rather Moola had it in all its beauty, and sold it to you, than that I should see the work of my hands spoilt. Keep it whole, and give it to Moola. I go, o King!'

With that Gron stumbled towards the door, but the King called him back.

'Return to your place, Gron,' he said in a kindly voice. 'The bird is yours. I would not spoil such loveliness. It was a test to find the rightful owner. I knew that he who made this golden bird would never wish to see it spoilt, even though he might lose it himself. Take it, Gron, and give it to your little daughter. And, in your spare time, make me another like it, and charge your own price. I will buy it from you when you please.'

Gron took the golden peacock, hardly able to believe his ears. Tears poured down his cheeks, and he could say no word. He had spent so much time, so much loving labour on the lovely bird, and it had grieved him to lose it. Now he could give it to his little daughter, as he had planned, and with loving care could fashion yet another peacock for the King himself. He was a proud and happy man.

But Moola shook with fear and turned as yellow as a ripe pear with fright.

'Take him to prison,' ordered the King.

'No, let him go, o King,' begged Gron, merciful in his happiness. 'I bear him no malice. Let him go.'

'You have beauty in your soul as well as in your clever hands!' said the King. 'Come to live at my court, Gron – I have need of such men as you.'

So Gron came to live at the court, and spent the rest of his long life happy in making the palace beautiful for his wise master, the King.

The Brownie and the Gnome

The brownie Beppy and the gnome Noggle were having a fierce quarrel. It was the gnome's fault. He said that the brownie had stolen the yellow brooch that he, Noggle, always wore in the front of his coat, and Beppy the brownie, who was a very honest little fellow, declared a hundred times that he hadn't!

'Well,' said Noggle fiercely, 'you were the only person walking with me when I missed the brooch, weren't you? We were walking through the woods together, and suddenly I felt the pin of my brooch open and the brooch fell – but when I looked on the ground for it, it wasn't there. So somehow or other, you, Beppy, must have picked it up and pocketed it!'

'I didn't, I didn't!' shouted Beppy, dancing about in a rage.

'Well, I warn you, Beppy,' said Noggle, pointing his finger at the brownie in a very nasty manner, 'I warn you – I shall come in the middle of one night and take something of *yours*. Yes, I shall! Something you like very much, just to pay you out for stealing my brooch. I expect I shall take your green necklace.'

'You won't, you shan't!' said Beppy angrily. 'Anyway, I shall hear you and chase you away.'

'I shall come so quietly that you won't hear a sound!' said Noggle. 'I shall get a Silent Spell from my aunt Dame Whispers. Then my feet won't make the tiniest noise at all.'

He did just what he said. He went to Dame Whispers and bought a Silent Spell, and then he planned to go to Beppy's and take his green necklace. He thought he had better wait until the moon was out of the sky, for the nights were just then very bright with moonlight. So he waited for six days and nights, and then decided to creep to the brownie's at midnight.

He looked at the little silver watch on his wrist. It was eleven o'clock. He would go in twenty minutes' time, then he would arrive at Beppy's just about the middle of the night when the brownie would be sound asleep. He wouldn't wake him because the Silent Spell would be in his feet, and they wouldn't make a single sound.

In twenty minutes' time he went to the door

and looked out. The night was very dark indeed. There wasn't even a small moon – in fact, the sky was so dark with clouds that Noggle felt certain it would soon rain. So he thought he would take his umbrella with him. He took it out of the hall-stand, looked at his watch again, and decided that it was time to start.

Out he went into the darkness, glad to think he was going to punish Beppy for stealing his brooch. It wasn't raining yet, so he didn't put up his umbrella. He walked along the lane, his feet making no sound at all. The Silent Spell was a very good one.

It was just midnight when he reached Beppy's cottage. Without a sound he opened a window and crept inside. He made his way up the stairs, without a single creak, to the brownie's bedroom. He opened the door and stood inside the room, listening to see if the brownie was asleep.

Beppy was asleep. He heard no sound of footsteps. He heard no creak. He heard no shuffling – but in his dreams he heard something else. His sharp little brownie ears heard the sound of a watch ticking! The watch that Noggle the gnome wore on his wrist had rather a loud tick, and the Silent Spell wasn't made for watches

– only for feet. So the watch ticked out in the darkness and came to the sleeping brownie's ears.

He woke up. He listened to the little tick-tick-tick that he could hear quite plainly. What could it be? It wasn't loud enough for a clock, and anyway, there wasn't a clock in the bedroom. It must be a watch. But Beppy had taken his watch to be mended that very day, so it couldn't be *his* watch ticking.

Then it must be someone else's – and that someone else must be standing in his bedroom in the dark! Ooh!

Beppy was just going to shout loudly when he thought:'Ah! It must be Noggle, come to steal my necklace! He has a Silent Spell in his feet, but he forgot about his watch! I'll give him a fright.'

Beppy sat up quietly in bed.

'I see you, Noggle,' he said, in an awful hollow voice. 'I see you. You're standing over there in the dark, thinking I can't see or hear you. But I can! And I'm going to put a spell on you! I'm going to turn on a tap behind you and make you wet from head to foot. Look out!'

As he spoke Beppy took up a glass of water by his bedside and threw the water at the corner where he could hear the tick-tick of the watch. It fell on Noggle's head and wetted him. He really thought a tap had been turned on behind him, and, howling in fright, he turned and ran down the stairs, almost falling over in his fear.

When he got outside it was pouring with rain. He put up his umbrella at once – and something fell out of it on to the ground. What could it be? Noggle lit a match and looked. Goodness, gracious, it was his little yellow brooch!

Noggle looked at it in surprise. Then he went very red. He guessed at once what had happened. When it had fallen from his coat in the wood, it had tumbled into his umbrella, and neither he nor Beppy had thought of looking there! So Beppy hadn't taken it after all!

'Beppy! Beppy! I've found my yellow brooch!' cried Noggle, rushing back into the cottage. 'It had fallen into my umbrella. I've just found it. Oh, do forgive me for being so nasty. And do tell me how you knew I was in your bedroom tonight.'

Beppy lit his lamp and the two looked at the yellow brooch. They began to laugh – and how they laughed! Noggle poked Beppy in the ribs and Beppy poked Noggle, and they teased one another and forgot all about their silly quarrel.

'Well, *next* time you want to come and take my green necklace, remember to leave your watch at home!' said Beppy. 'I heard it ticking and that's how I knew you were there!'

'There won't be any next time,' said Noggle. 'We'll be good friends now.'

And so they are!'

The Inside-out Stocking

Once there was a little boy called Rex, who was always having bad luck. People were quite sorry for him because he was so unlucky.

If he ran too fast he fell down and hurt his knee. If he climbed into a swing, he soon fell out. If he had a pound given to him, it was lost through a hole in his pocket. That was the kind of little boy he was.

There was one thing he was very good at, and that was running races. He could run really fast, and could beat anyone if only he didn't catch his foot against something and tumble over! He wasn't good at jumping, and he wasn't good at swimming, but it really was marvellous to see him run.

Now in the field near his home a sports day was going to be held. All the schools of the town were to meet there and see which one was the best at running, jumping, slow bicycle racing, obstacle races and other things. It would be great fun.

'I hope you will win the running race for us,' said the headmaster of his school to Rex. 'You ought to, my boy, for you are a splendid runner for your age.'

'I'll do my best, sir,' answered Rex, 'but I'm a very unlucky person, you know. I never win anything. I'm always losing things, or hurting myself, or getting into trouble. I can't seem to help it!'

'Rex is sure to get measles or mumps on the day of the race!' said one of the bigger boys. 'He caught chicken-pox on Christmas Day. He has no luck at all!'

Now Rex had a small sister called Lucy, who loved him very much indeed. She was quite a lucky little person, and she was always very sad because Rex was so unlucky. Just fancy, he hadn't even been able to go to the seaside in the holidays because he had broken his leg and had to go away to hospital!

Lucy was always afraid of what might happen next to Rex. She hardly dared to plan anything nice for him in case something unlucky happened. She was very pleased when she heard about the sports day, for she felt sure that if only Rex were able to run in the race he would win it, for certain! But suppose it was another of his unlucky days?

'I *do* wish I could make certain sure that Rex would have a lucky day instead of an unlucky day on the sports day!' thought Lucy. 'I think I'll go and see old Mother Brown, who lives in that funny little cottage at the end of our village. People say she is very old and very wise, so perhaps she could tell me how to help Rex.'

The very next day she went. She took with her an egg laid by her own little white hen to give to Mother Brown. The old lady was very pleased and told Lucy to sit down in the big rocking-chair.

'Mother Brown, could you tell me how a person can be lucky?' asked Lucy, rocking herself to and fro in the big chair.

'Well, a black cat brings luck,' said Mother Brown. Lucy thought that was no use to her because there were no black cats near her home.

'What else?' she asked the old woman.

'Well, a piece of white heather is lucky,' said Mother Brown. That was no use to Lucy either, for no heather of any sort grew near her village.

'Then, of course, it's lucky if you get up in the morning and put on your stocking inside-out without noticing,' said Mother Brown. 'That's really very lucky – only most people notice what they're doing and turn their stocking the right way out.'

Lucy's eyes brightened. Ah, here was something she could do! Suppose she crept into her brother's bedroom the night before the sports and turned one of his stockings inside-out! If he didn't notice it, it might make him very lucky that day and he would win the race. She would try it!

So on the night before the sports day Lucy lay wide awake in bed, waiting for Rex to fall asleep. When she thought he really *must* be asleep she crept into his room and quickly turned one of his stockings inside-out. Then back to bed she scampered and soon fell asleep herself.

The next morning Lucy looked anxiously at Rex to see if his stocking was on inside-out. It was! He had put it on without noticing it. Lucy was full of delight. Now what would happen?

Everything went smoothly that day. Rex was happy, and felt certain he was going to win the race. He and Lucy went to the sports field at the right time and stood there waiting to be told what to do. Then suddenly Lucy heard one of the teachers talking.

'Look at that boy over there! He's got his stocking on inside-out! How careless of him. It looks very untidy. Lucy, you're his sister, aren't you? Go and tell him to change his stocking and put it right. Quickly, or there will be no time!'

Poor Lucy! She didn't know what to do. Then she made up her mind that whatever happened, she wouldn't take away Rex's luck. She ran up to him, and instead of telling him about his stocking, she whispered to him to go away to the other side of the field with her. Off they went, and the teacher who had sent her to Rex watched them both in annoyance. Whatever was that naughty little Lucy doing?

But the races were beginning! First one race and then another – the jumping – then the slow bicycle race – then the egg and spoon race – and whatever do you think, Rex won that! He didn't drop his egg once, and he was so surprised and pleased.

He won the running race too! Once he stumbled and almost fell – but not quite! He finished well ahead of all the other children and everyone clapped and cheered loudly. Lucy clapped loudest of all.

'Well, wasn't I lucky today!' cried Rex, very pleased and proud. 'I can't think what happened to me! I really can't. Look at my running prize, Lucy – a fine football. You and I will have plenty of good games with it! I saw your excited

face when I was running that race. I shouldn't
be surprised if you brought me luck!'

Lucy didn't tell him what she had done. His
stocking was still inside-out, and he didn't know
it!

'I'll creep into his room each time I want him
to have a lucky day, and turn one of his
stockings inside-out again,' thought the little
girl. 'I mustn't tell him or he might notice
another time. How lovely that I know a lucky
trick like that!'

I think she was rather a nice little girl, don't
you? Rex often has lucky days now, and he can't
think why. But I can!

The Clockwork Mouse
and the Bird

In the toy-cupboard lived a clockwork mouse and a pecking-bird. The clockwork mouse was a dear little thing, and ran all over the floor when he was wound up. But the pecking-bird was a tiresome nuisance.

He was supposed to peck up crumbs from the floor, but instead of that he pecked the other toys! He thought it was very funny to do that. He used to get the old red duck to wind him up and then off he would go, peck-peck-peck, nipping the teddy-bear, pecking the curly-haired doll and jabbing the railway train.

One day he pecked the clockwork mouse and nipped a big piece of fur from his back. It left a bare patch, and the mouse was cross.

'What do you think you're doing?' he cried angrily. 'Leave me alone! See what a nasty bald place you have given me! You are a great nuisance!'

The pecking-bird laughed, and nipped the

little mouse again. Peck! Another bit of fur flew off, and the mouse squeaked in pain. Peck! This time the pecking-bird nipped at the mouse's key and it flew out of his side. The pecking-bird ran after the key, pecked at it, and swallowed it!

Now whatever do you think of that? Wasn't that a dreadful thing to do? The toys all stared at the pecking-bird in horror, because, as you can guess, it is a terrible thing to lose your key if you happen to be clockwork. It means you don't work any more – you can't move, or walk, or run, or peck, or whatever it is you do when you are wound up.

'Where's my key?' squealed the clockwork mouse in excitement. 'Where is it? Give it back to me, you wicked pecking-bird!'

'I can't,' said the pecking-bird, pleased. 'It's inside me!'

The teddy-bear thumped the pecking-bird on his back, hoping to make him choke and cough up the key. But it only gave him hiccups, and the key stayed inside him.

The little mouse wept so many tears that his feet were wet with standing in the tear-puddle he made. The toys were very, very sorry for him, and very angry with the unkind pecking-bird. But they really didn't know what to do, because they were all half afraid of the pecking-bird.

Then the brown toy dog had a wonderful idea. He called the toys into a corner and whispered to them.

'Have you ever noticed,' he said, 'that the key of the pecking-bird always looked just the same as the key of the clockwork mouse? Suppose, just suppose, that the bird's key fits the mouse? Wouldn't that be grand? Then we could give the mouse the key and the pecking-bird wouldn't have one – except inside him, where it wouldn't be any use!'

'Ooh!' said all the toys, in delight. 'We'll wait till the pecking-bird is asleep and then we'll slip his key out of him and try it in the clockwork mouse!'

So when the pecking-bird stood fast asleep in a corner the teddy-bear crept up to him and carefully pulled out his key. Then he hurried up to the waiting clockwork mouse.

It fitted! Yes, it really did! Quickly the bear wound up the mouse and the little creature ran merrily over the nursery floor. The pecking-bird heard him and woke up.

He stared in astonishment at the mouse. Then he called to his friend, the red duck. 'Duck, come and wind me up quickly! I'm going to peck that noisy mouse! How dare he get another key!'

The duck waddled up. She looked first this side of the pecking-bird and then the other.

'I don't see your key,' she said, puzzled.

'Don't be silly!' said the bird impatiently. 'Are you blind? Look closer and you'll see it sticking out.'

'Indeed, I see nothing but a hole where it went,' said the red duck.

Then the pecking-bird became anxious and looked himself – and to his great dismay he saw that his key was indeed gone.

'Where's my key?' he screamed.

'I've got it, I've got it!' squeaked the mouse in delight and ran right up to the pecking-bird to show him.

'You thief!' cried the pecking-bird, trying to peck. But of course he couldn't move his head at all. He wasn't wound up.

'No more thief than you are!' answered the mouse. 'You took my key, and I've got yours. Fair exchange is no robbery, you know! Ho, ho, what a joke! You've got my key inside you and you can't use it!'

'It serves you right!' said the teddy-bear. 'You

were always unkind, pecking-bird, and now you can't be horrid any more. If you hadn't taken the mouse's key this would never have happened. You can just stand in your corner now and be forgotten.'

So there stands the pecking-bird in his corner, never moving. But they do say that every now and again the kind-hearted little clockwork mouse takes out his key and puts it into the pecking-bird. Then for a little time the bird comes to life again – but he is not alllowed to keep the key for long! No – the toys don't trust him, and I don't blame them, do you?

The Spotted Cow

There was once rather a vain cow. She was plain white with two nice curly horns. She thought she looked rather nice – but she did wish she could have some nice black spots over her back. There were no spotted cows in the field at all, and the white cow thought it would be grand to be the only spotted cow.

Now one day, when she was munching the long, juicy grass that grew in the hedge, she came across a small pixie mixing black paint in a pot.

'What are you doing?' asked the cow.

'I'm mixing my black paint,' said the little fellow. 'I'm the pixie that paints the spots on the ladybirds, you know.'

'Oh!' said the cow. 'Well, will you paint some on me?'

'Yes, if you'll give me a nice drink of milk,' said the pixie.

'I don't mind doing that,' said the cow. 'You

can find a tin mug, and milk some of my creamy milk into it for yourself.'

'I'll just finish these ladybirds first,' said the pixie, and he turned back to his work. In a long line stood about twenty ladybirds with bright red backs and no spots. The pixie neatly painted seven black spots on each red back, and the ladybirds flew off in delight.

When he had finished his work he looked at the waiting cow. 'I'll go and find my mug,' he said. 'I'm very thirsty, and I'd love a drink of your nice milk.'

He ran off and came back with a mug. On it was his name: 'Pixie Pinnie'. He milked the cow, and took a mugful of her creamy milk. Then he began to mix some more black paint.

'Are you sure you'd like *black* spots?' he asked. 'You wouldn't like a few blue ones, or red ones? You would look most uncommon then.'

The cow thought about it. 'No,' she said at last. 'I don't think so. I'd rather have black spots. They will look smarter than coloured ones.'

'Well, you must stand still,' said the pixie, 'or I might smudge the spots, and that would look horrid. Now then – are you ready?'

The pixie began to paint the cow. Goodness,

you should have seen him! A big black spot here, and a little one there! Two by her tail, and three down her back. Four in a ring on her nose, and a whole crowd of spots down her sides. She *did* look grand!

At last the pixie had finished. He put away his paints, took another drink of milk, and said 'goodbye'. The cow left him and went back to the field. How grand she felt!

The other cows stared at her. They didn't know her. Who was this funny spotted cow?

'Don't you know me?' said the cow, proudly. 'I've grown spots.'

'Rubbish!' said the biggest cow. 'Grown spots, indeed. You don't belong to us. Go away, you horrid, spotted creature, we don't want anything to do with you!'

Just then the little boy who looked after the cows came along to see if they were all right. When he saw the spotted one he stared in surprise.

'You're not one of our cows,' he said. 'You must have wandered in here from somewhere else. You had better get out of the field, and go back to your own meadow, wherever it is! What an ugly, spotted creature you are! I'm glad you're not one of *our* cows!'

He opened the gate and pushed the surprised cow out. She trotted down the lane angrily. 'I'll go to the next field,' she thought. 'The cows there will be pleased to have such a fine spotted creature as I am!'

But they weren't pleased! They mooed at her and sent her away. She was very miserable.

'I wish I hadn't got spots now,' she thought to herself. 'It was a mistake. I'll find that pixie, and ask him to take them away.'

But he was gone. She couldn't see him anywhere. Then it began to rain. The cow stood under a tree to shelter herself, but the rain was so heavy that she was soon wet from horn to tail – and, dear me, the black spots all came out in the rain! Soon there were none left at all.

The cow didn't know that the rain had washed the black spots away. She stood there, feeling lonely and miserable, and when the rain had stopped she made up her mind to go back to her own field, and ask the other cows to have her back again. So off she went, whisking her big tail from side to side.

The little boy was still there. He saw her as she came, and now that she had no spots, he knew her for one of his own cows. So he opened the gate, and let her through, saying: 'Dear me,

wherever have you been?'

The other cows crowded round her, for, now that she had no spots, they knew her too.

'We are glad to see you,' they said. 'Do you know, a horrible spotted cow came in your place, and said she was you. She's gone now, thank goodness. Ugly creature that she was! How dared she say she was you, for you are so white and pretty!'

The cow didn't say anything. She listened and hung her head. It was better to be white and pretty than to be handsome and spotted. She didn't look so grand now, but she was herself.

'I hope that pixie doesn't give me away,' she thought. 'The cows *will* laugh at me, if he does!'

But I don't expect he will!

The Cross Caterpillar

Once upon a time there was a little green and yellow caterpillar who lived on a big green cabbage with his brothers and sisters. He hadn't been very long hatched out of an egg but he didn't know that. He was just a bit bigger than the others, and he thought himself very grand indeed.

He ate all day long. He chose the tenderest and juiciest bit of cabbage for himself, and was very angry if another caterpillar dared to share it. He would stand up on his tail end then and look very fierce indeed.

He grew bigger and bigger. He had a few hairs on him here and there, and as he grew bigger they grew longer. He was an artful caterpillar too. He knew quite well that if a shadow came across the cabbage it might be a bird hunting for caterpillars and then he would huddle into a crinkle of the cabbage and keep as still as a stalk. Some of his brothers and sisters were eaten, but not the artful caterpillar. Oh, no, he was far too clever.

One day, when he was quite big, a pretty fluttering creature came to the cabbage. It was a white butterfly with black spots. It sat down on the cabbage and waved its feelers about. The caterpillar peered over the edge of the cabbage leaf and looked at it. When it saw that it was a mild and harmless-looking creature, the caterpillar flew into a temper and cried, 'Get off my cabbage! I was just going to eat this leaf!'

'Gently, gently!' said the butterfly, looking at the cross caterpillar. 'This is as much my cabbage as yours, caterpillar.'

'It certainly isn't!' said the caterpillar, standing up on his hind legs and waving himself about. But the butterfly was not at all frightened. It opened and closed its lovely white wings and laughed.

'You don't know what you are talking about,' said the butterfly. 'I have come to lay my eggs here. I shall lay them on the underneath of the leaf you are sitting on. It is, as you have found out, a tender, juicy leaf, fit for my eggs.'

The caterpillar was as angry as could be. The butterfly took no notice of it at all. She began to lay neat little rows of eggs in exactly the place where the caterpillar had planned to eat his dinner. It was too bad!

'Now don't you dare to touch my eggs!' said the butterfly, warningly, as she flew off. 'If you do, I'll tell the pixie who lives by the wall, and she will come and spank you!'

The caterpillar was so angry that he couldn't say a word. But after a while he found his voice and began to talk to the others about it.

'Brother and sister caterpillars,' he said. 'We cannot stand this. Why should those horrid, ugly, flapping butterflies come and steal our cabbage for their silly eggs? Why should they be allowed to laugh at us and do what they like? Is not this our cabbage? Let us eat all these eggs up.'

'Oh, no!' cried the listening caterpillars. 'If we do that the pixie will come along, as the butterfly said, and she might be very cross indeed.'

Just as the caterpillar was opening his mouth to talk again two more white butterflies came up, and when they saw the nice, juicy cabbage they at once began to lay eggs there. The caterpillar was so angry that he rushed at them and tried to push them off. But they flapped their big wings in his face and scared him. When they had gone he sat down and thought hard.

'*I* will go to the pixie who lives by the wall!' he said. 'Yes, I will. I will complain of these horrid, interfering butterflies, and I will ask the pixie to catch them all and keep them in a cage. Then they can do no more mischief to our cabbage!'

'That is a fine idea!' said all the caterpillars, stopping their eating for a moment. 'Go now.'

So the green caterpillar left his cabbage and crawled down the path to the pixie who lived by the wall. She was most surprised to see him.

'I have come to complain of those hateful butterflies who interfere with our cabbage,' said the caterpillar.

'Which butterflies?' asked the pixie in astonishment.

'The white ones with black spots,' said the caterpillar, fiercely. 'I want you to catch them all and keep them in a cage so that they can do no more harm to our cabbage.'

The pixie laughed and laughed, and the caterpillar felt crosser and crosser as he watched her. At last she dried her eyes and said: 'Well, I will promise to do what you say if you will come to me in four weeks' time and ask me again. I will certainly do what you want then.'

The caterpillar went away, content. In four weeks' time all those horrid butterflies would be caught and put in a cage. Ah, that would teach them to come interfering with his cabbage! He was pleased, and proud of himself. He began to eat his cabbage again and in two days he had grown simply enormous.

Then a strange feeling came over him. He wanted to sleep. He was no longer hungry. He felt strange. Some of his brothers and sisters felt sleepy too, and one day they all fell asleep, having first hung themselves up neatly in silken hammocks. They all turned into chrysalides, and kept as still as if they were dead.

After some time they woke up. Our caterpillar awoke first, for he was strong and big. He wanted to get out of the chrysalis bed he was in, so he bit a hole and crawled out. The sun was warm and he stretched himself. He seemed bigger and lighter. How strange!

He saw a white butterfly in the air and at once all his anger came back to him. He would go to the pixie by the wall, for it must surely now be four weeks since he had seen her, and he would make her keep her promise! He set out to walk as he had done before – but to his great amazement he found himself floating in the air.

He screwed his head round and looked at himself. He was flying! Yes, he had four lovely white wings, spotted with black. He was a butterfly!

'I am lovely!' he thought in delight. 'I am a beautiful creature! Look at my fine wings! Oh, how happy I am!'

He flew about in the air, enjoying the sunshine. Suddenly he heard a small voice calling to him and he saw the pixie who lived by the wall. She knew him even though he was no longer a caterpillar.

'Have you come to ask me to keep my promise?' she asked, with a little tinkling laugh. 'I am quite ready to keep it! And the butterfly I will catch first and keep in a cage shall be *you*!'

The butterfly was frightened. He flew high in the air. How foolish he had been! No wonder the pixie had laughed! But how in the world was he to know that one day he would change from a green caterpillar to a white butterfly?

'I am not so wise as I thought I was,' said the butterfly to himself. 'I know nothing! I will be quiet and gentle in future, and I will never lose my temper again!'

Where is he now? In your garden and mine looking for a little butterfly wife to marry – and you may be sure he will say to her, 'Lay your eggs on a cabbage leaf, my dear! It's the best thing to do – and don't you mind what the rude and stupid caterpillars say to you – they don't know anything at all!'

What a Mistake!

Once upon a time the King of Gnomeland had a lovely garden, kept neat and pretty by twenty-one gardeners. The head gardener was a fat and surly gnome called Gurgle. He was a good gardener, but most unpleasant to the gnomes who worked under him. How he scolded them! And never a word of praise did he give them when they did anything good.

They all disliked him, and feared him. He had a horrid habit of creeping round corners very suddenly and pouncing on them to see if they were doing their work properly. He frightened them so much that they dropped whatever they were carrying, and I couldn't tell you how many pots were broken because of Gurgle's sly ways.

Now Gurgle had a special pair of garden scissors that he was very fond of. They were large and sharp, and most comfortable to hold. They were usually kept hanging in the garden shed, and, dear me, wasn't Gurgle angry if anyone borrowed them!

One day the King himself wandered into the shed and saw them. He thought they would be just the thing for cutting off a piece of rose tree that knocked against his bedroom window. So he borrowed them.

And, of course, it *would* happen that Gurgle came along that same afternoon and wanted them himself. When he found that they were not in the shed he was very angry indeed.

He went round roaring and grumbling, and even when he discovered that it was the King himself who had borrowed them, he didn't stop roaring.

'Those are *my* scissors!' he cried. 'I won't have anyone borrowing them, not even the King, that I won't. I'll keep them safely somewhere so that no one can borrow them!'

And where do you think he kept them when he got them back? He had a special hat made, and instead of putting a feather into it he put his scissors!

Now Gurgle had a very bad memory indeed. He quite forgot that he had put his scissors into his hat that afternoon, and he went to the garden shed to get them from their usual place. And, of course, they weren't there! How annoying! How aggravating! How very, very vexing!

He began to roar and rage as usual, and everyone came running to see what was the matter.

'My scissors have gone again!' he shouted. 'Who has taken them?'

'Please sir,' said a small gnome, nervously, 'you took them yourself and they . . .'

'I TOOK THEM MYSELF!' shouted the gnome in anger. 'How ridiculous to say a thing like that when I'm looking for them. If I took them myself I'd have them in my hands, wouldn't I?'

'But sir, you've got . . .' began the little gnome, trembling. Gurgle wouldn't let him finish.

'How dare you argue with me!' he roared. 'Go and dig for six hours in the kitchen garden for a punishment.'

Well, of course, nobody else dared say a word after that. They all stood silently round Gurgle, looking at the scissors stuck in his hat, and wishing that Gurgle would remember they were there.

'Now then, who's borrowed them?' roared Gurgle in a fury. 'Whoever it is had better own up before I punish him very, VERY severely. I've got this punishment all written out here and the head cook has promised to come and read it out if I don't get my scissors back at once.'

Nobody said anything at all. Nobody dared to. They stared at Gurgle, wondering whatever was going to happen.

Gurgle clapped his hands. The head cook came running down the path. He was not a nice fellow and the little gnomes didn't like him very much. He was only too pleased to read out a dreadful punishment, and see it happen to one of the gnome gardeners.

'Cook, someone has got my scissors again,' said Gurgle, angrily. 'Will you please stand in the middle of us and read out the punishment. I will stand here and watch to see who the gardener is, and I shall box his ears when I know!'

The head cook cleared his throat and looked at the paper Gurgle handed him. Then he began to read, slowly and loudly. This is what he read:

'Now hear the dreadful punishment for the one who has my scissors at this very moment. May his ears grow long like donkey's ears! May his hair fall out! May his nails grow as long as a tiger's claws! May his nose shoot out like a snake! May . . .'

Gurgle looked round to see who was the
gnome to have such a dreadful punishment –
and to his surprise no one seemed to change at
all! But what was this? Oh, goodness, gracious,
what was happening to his ears? To his hair,
that was dropping down all round him; to his
nails, and to his nose! Oh, his poor nose! It grew
as long as a snake and waved about in the air!

Gurgle gave such a shriek that the head cook
stopped reading and looked at him in surprise.
When he saw what had happened he dropped
his paper, began to shake like a leaf, and then
ran back to his kitchen as fast as his legs could
carry him, crying, 'He's got the scissors in his
hat! He's got the scissors in his hat! Oooooooooh
my!'

The gnome gardeners stared at Gurgle with
wide eyes. Then they began to laugh. They
couldn't help it. Gurgle looked so funny – and to
think he had brought his own punishment on
himself, too!

'Ho, ho, ho,' they roared. 'Ho, ho, ho!'

The King heard all the noise and came to see
what the matter was. When he saw Gurgle
standing there looking such a dreadful sight,
with tears pouring down his long nose, he didn't
know *what* to say.

At last he asked one of the gnomes to explain everything to him, and the little gnome, stammering and trying not to laugh, told the King all that had happened.

The King listened, frowning.

'You are an unkind gnome, Gurgle,' he said, 'to think of such a fearful punishment for someone whose only fault was that they had borrowed your scissors. Why, I myself might have borrowed them again, and this spell would have worked on *me* then. Well, you are certainly well-punished, Gurgle, and I shall do nothing about it. Keep your long ears, your long nails, your long nose and your bald head! It will help you to remember that bad temper and spitefulness always come back to the owner, and harm him more than they harm anybody else!'

So there is Gurgle, humble and ashamed, hoping and hoping that one day he will become his own self once more. He tries to be sweet-tempered, he tries to be fair, and sooner or later he will grow right again. But it is a long time to wait.

What a mistake!

The Cookie Swan

Once upon a time a little girl called Sallie asked a friend to tea.

'Will there be jam and cakes for tea?' Sallie asked her mother.

'You can have some strawberry jam, and I will make you a cookie swan,' said her mother. Sallie was pleased. Her mother could make lovely cookie swans, white, with a black currant eye each side. They swam upright on a cake-plate and looked very grand indeed.

The cookie swan that day was the nicest and best you ever saw. It was so good that when Mother put it upright on a blue dish, the teapot and the jug both cried out in admiration.

'You are just like a real swan!' said the teapot, in a steamy voice.

'You are beautiful,' said the milk jug, in a creamy voice.

'I am a swan,' said the cookie swan, and he actually spread out his wings.

'You're not a *real* swan,' said the teapot. 'You are only a cookie swan.'

'There's no difference,' said the foolish swan. 'A swan is a swan no matter what it is made of.'

'Ah, but there *is* a difference,' said the milk jug, in its rich voice. 'A real swan swims for years on the river, but a cookie swan only lasts a day.'

'How do you mean, only lasts a day?' asked the cookie swan in surprise.

'Well, you are made to be eaten,' said the teapot and milk jug together. 'When Sallie comes in with her friend they will eat you.'

The cookie swan opened his currant eyes wide with fear when he heard this. He had thought himself very grand indeed, and it was dreadful to be told that he was only made to be eaten.

At that moment Sallie and her little friend came running in. Sallie looked at the tea-table and when she saw the big cookie swan swimming proudly on its blue dish she gave a squeal of delight.

'Look!' she said. 'Mother has made us a beautiful cookie swan. You shall eat the head and tail, Lizzie, and I will eat the middle.'

But this was more than the cookie swan could bear. He suddenly flapped his wings and flew straight off the table. When he got to the floor he found his legs and tore off as fast as he could. Sallie shouted when she saw him go.

'Cookie swan, cookie swan, come back and be eaten!'

But the cookie swan only went all the faster, and although Sallie ran after him at top speed he was soon out of sight. He used his wings as well as his legs, and as he went he muttered: 'I won't be gobbled up, I won't, I won't!'

He ran out into the yard where there were many brown and white hens pecking at the ground. They saw him and gazed in surprise. Then the big cock rushed after him, seeing he was a cookie.

'Cookie swan, cookie swan, come back and be eaten!' he crowed.

But the swan only went all the faster, and no matter how fast the cock ran, he couldn't catch the swan. 'I won't be gobbled up, I won't, I won't!' cried the swan as he went down the yard.

He slipped under a gate and came to the pig-sty. The pig was there, rooting in his straw. When he saw the cookie he raised up his snout and sniffed. It smelt good. The pig trotted up to the cookie, who was standing panting for breath by the gate.

The swan saw the pig just in time, and opening his wings, he flew up to the third bar of the gate just out of the pig's reach.

'Cookie swan, cookie swan, come back and be eaten!' grunted the pig.

But the swan wouldn't. He flew up into the air and flapped his way into a dark stable, crying, 'I won't be gobbled up, I won't, I won't!' Inside was a horse, chewing hay from a manger. The swan settled beside him trembling. The horse stopped his chewing and looked in surprise at the swan. A smell of cookie reached his big brown nose and he put back his upper lip to snatch at the swan. But the swan flew down to the ground and ran between his big shaggy hoofs to the door.

'Cookie swan, cookie swan, come back and be eaten!' neighed the horse, disappointed. He tried to go after the swan, but the lower part of the stable door was shut and he could not go out. He stood looking over the top at the cookie swan who was flapping about outside.

'I won't be gobbled up, I won't, I won't!' screeched the cookie swan, as he flapped his cookie wings.

The swan didn't know where to go. Everywhere he went there seemed to be creatures that wanted to eat him. It was dreadful.

Then, away in the distance he saw the duck pond. There were white ducks on it, swimming and diving. It all looked very peaceful and pretty.

'That's the place for me,' said the cookie swan to himself. 'I'll go to the pond and swim about with the ducks. That is what a real swan does, and I will be a real swan. I will not be a cookie swan, made to be eaten!'

So off he went, half running, half flying to the duck pond. He flopped into the water and tried to swim. But cookie swans are not really meant to swim, and he found himself gradually falling over on one side. Splash! He lay quite on his side, one eye in the water. He could not raise himself upright no matter how he tried.

'Help, help!' he cried, as he struggled. A big duck came swimming up at once.

'What's the matter?' she asked.

'I'm a swan and I've come to swim here,' said the cookie swan. 'But I've fallen on my side, and something horrid is happening to me.'

So there was. He was slowly falling to bits in the water. Poor cookie swan!

'If you like, I'll put my beak into the water and you can climb on to it,' said the duck.

'Oh, thank you,' cried the swan. So the duck put her beak into the water and the poor cookie swan scrambled up on it. Then the duck lifted up her beak and began to swim to shore with the swan balanced carefully across it.

But the other ducks saw that this duck was carrying something and they swam after her, quacking loudly. They tried to snap the cookie swan away, and the duck, opening her mouth to quack angrily, found the cookie swan falling down her throat. Oh, what a delicious mouthful! The duck swallowed joyfully, and the cookie swan disappeared.

But as he went, he cried: 'I won't be gobbled up, I won't, I won't!'

And, you know, he never knew he was, so he was quite happy to the very last moment!

Why Did the Giant Laugh?

There was once a kind-hearted giant called Whopping. He was just like his name, simply enormous, with a great big head, long, strong arms, and legs that could stride miles without getting tired.

He was a good-natured creature, and most people liked him. He was gardener to the Lord High Chamberlain of Brownieland, and a very good one he made too, for he could dig twice as fast and twice as much as ten men at once! He could sweep up leaves in a second with his enormous broom, and could carry great loads of bricks or earth in his big barrow. The other gardeners did the planting and the weeding, for Whopping's hands were too big to handle small things. But he loved doing the big things.

Now one day, as he was going home wheeling his big barrow, whom did he see but Mr Dunce and his wife, walking slowly along the road,

each carrying a heavy sack, full of carrots and
onions for soup.

They had been a long way and they were tired.
Whopping felt sorry for them. They lived next
door to him, and by the time they reached home
he would have had his meal, read his paper,
undressed and gone to bed! But then, his long
legs took him twice as fast over the fields as Mr
Dunce's thin ones and his wife's little fat ones.

The kind-hearted giant stopped and called to
the tired couple.

'Hi!' he called. 'Hi, Mr Dunce and Mrs
Dunce! Want a lift?'

'Oh, thank you,' said Mr Dunce, looking
round. 'But what in?'

'My big wheelbarrow, of course,' said
Whopping, laughing. 'It's quite clean, and I can
easily take you both. We'll be home in no time!'

'Well, thank you very much,' said Mr and
Mrs Dunce. They climbed into the wheelbarrow
and sat down side by side. 'We do hope we
shan't be too heavy for you.'

'Not a bit, not a bit!' said Whopping. Mr
Dunce whispered something to his wife, and they
both solemnly lifted up their sacks of onions and
carrots and put them on their shoulders.

'What do you want to do that for?' asked

Whopping in surprise. 'Why don't you put your sacks beside you in the barrow? You don't want to be bowed down under their weight all the way home.'

'Oh,' said Mr Dunce, 'we thought perhaps it would be too much for you, carrying us and our heavy sacks too. So I told my wife to put her sack on her shoulder and carry it herself, and I did the same with mine. Then, you see, you would only have *us* to carry, and not our sacks, too.'

Whopping listened and then he roared with laughter. How he laughed! Really, all the trees shook as if they were in a big wind when his laugh went roaring down the road! As for Mr and Mrs Dunce they looked quite offended.

'What's the joke?' asked Mr Dunce, stiffly. 'I don't see anything to laugh at in what I have just said.'

Whopping tried to explain that the two sillies and their sacks were all in the barrow, whether they carried the sacks on their shoulders or not, but he laughed so much that he couldn't say a word. Tears came into his eyes and two of them dropped down Mrs Dunce's neck.

She put up her umbrella at once and sat in the barrow looking most disgusted.

'Rude fellow!' she said to her husband. 'Isn't he an unmannerly, noisy, vulgar fellow, this giant? What does he want to laugh like that for, when you simply make an ordinary remark?'

'I'm sure I don't know,' said Mr Dunce, in a huff. 'A pretty sight we must look sitting in his barrow, and him roaring with laughter behind us as if we were a couple of clowns at a circus! I've a good mind to get out and walk.'

'No, don't let's do that, because my feet are tired,' said Mrs Dunce. 'It doesn't make any difference to him to have us in his barrow, a great, strong fellow like that! Why, I expect he could take ten of us and not feel it.'

Whopping still went on laughing every time he saw the two sacks so carefully perched up on the narrow shoulders of Mr and Mrs Dunce. At last Mr Dunce became very angry indeed, because every time Whopping laughed a great draught blew down Mr Dunce's neck, and he felt sure he would have a sore throat the next day.

He whispered to his wife.

'Wife, put down your sack in the barrow. I will do the same. If the giant is so horrid as to laugh at us for being kind enough to carry our heavy sacks ourselves, he deserves to be punished. He shall now carry our sacks for us as well as ourselves!'

Whopping heard what Mr Dunce said. He saw the little man put down his heavy sack into the barrow and Mrs Dunce did the same. The giant began to laugh all over again. It was too funny, really!

'What are you laughing at now?' asked Mr Dunce, in a temper.

But Whopping couldn't tell him; he was laughing too much. More tears fell out of his eyes and splashed on to Mr Dunce's head. He wiped them off with his handkerchief and spoke loudly to his wife. 'I wish I had brought my mackintosh with me,' he said.

That made Whopping laugh more than ever, and suddenly the barrow tipped over and the two Dunces fell out, sacks and all.

'Oh, dear, I'm so sorry,' said Whopping. 'But really, you shouldn't say such ridiculous things and make me laugh.'

Mr and Mrs Dunce picked up their sacks and walked away huffily. 'You *see*!' said Mr Dunce to his wife. 'As soon as we put our sacks down in the barrow, he wasn't strong enough to carry us and the sacks too, and tipped us out!'

At that Whopping began to roar again, and

the Dunces hurried away as fast as they could. Whether Whopping managed to get home that night or not I have never heard – but I do know that Mr and Mrs Dunce can't guess to this day why Whopping laughed so much! Can you?

Twinkle Gets into Mischief

Twinkle was a mischievous elf if ever there was one! You wouldn't believe the things he did – all the naughtiest things his quick little mind could think of. But one day he went too far, and tried to play tricks on Snorty the Dragon.

Twinkle wasn't afraid of anyone or anything, so when he heard that Snorty the Dragon was looking for someone brave enough to go and paint his cave walls a nice cheerful pink, he thought he would try to get the job. So off he went, carrying a fine big pot of pink paint, whistling gaily as he skipped along.

'Hello!' he said to Snorty, when he got to the cave. 'I hear you want your walls painted a pleasant pink.'

'Quite right,' said Snorty, blowing out some blue smoke from his nostrils.

'That's a clever trick!' said Twinkle. 'I wish I could blow smoke out of *my* nose!'

'Only dragons can do that!' said Snorty

proudly. 'And look at these!'

He suddenly shot out five enormous claws from each foot – but Twinkle didn't turn a hair.

'Splendid!' he said. 'But what a business it must be for you to cut your nails, Snorty! I should think you would need a pair of shears instead of scissors!'

The dragon didn't like being laughed at. He was used to frightening people, not amusing them. So he glared at Twinkle, and blew a flame out of his mouth.

'Ho, *you* don't need matches to light the gas!' chuckled Twinkle.

'That's not funny,' said Snorty sulkily. 'Get on with my painting, please, and make the walls a bright pink. And no more of your cheek, mind!'

'No more of my *tongue*, you mean!' said Twinkle, who did love having the last word. He began to mix his paint and to daub the wall with the bright pink colour. The dragon walked out in a huff and left him to it.

The cave was large and it took Twinkle all the day to do even half of it. When night came there was still half left to do. So he made up his mind to do it the next day. Snorty came back, and ate a sackful of corn for his supper. He liked the pink wall very much.

'Have you heard me roar?' he asked the elf suddenly, longing to give the cheeky little creature a real fright.

'No,' said Twinkle. 'Do roar a bit.'

So the dragon roared his loudest. Well, if you can imagine ten good thunderstorms, mixed up with a thousand dustbin-lids all crashing to the ground at once, and about five hundred dinner-plates breaking at the same time, you can guess a little bit what the dragon's roaring was like. It was really immense.

'What do you think of that?' asked Snorty, when he had finished.

'Well,' said Twinkle, 'how do you expect me to hear you roar when you just whisper like that? I could hardly hear you!'

The dragon was so angry at this cheeky speech that he lifted Twinkle up and opened his mouth and blew smoke all over him. That made the elf angry, and he ran into a corner, very red in the face, making up his mind to play a trick on the dragon the very first chance he had!

The dragon went to bed, and soon the awful sound of his snoring filled the cave. Twinkle couldn't possibly go to sleep, so he looked round for something naughty to do – and he saw the dragon's two pet geese at the end of the cave, their heads tucked under their wings. They were fine birds, as white as snow.

'Ha!' said Twinkle at once. 'I'll paint them pink. That will give old Snorty a fine shock in the morning!'

So he woke up the geese and painted the two surprised birds a brilliant pink. They looked very strange when they were finished. Then Twinkle looked round for something else to paint. He saw the dragon's cat, a great black creature, snoozing by the fire. What fun it would be to give it a pink tail and pink whiskers!

No sooner said than done! Twinkle dipped the cat's whiskers into his paint-pot and then dipped in the tail. What a dreadful sight the poor cat looked!

But that wasn't enough for Twinkle – no, he must do something even more daring than that! He would paint the dragon's beautiful brown tail! So he stole up to the snoring dragon and painted his tail a vivid pink from beginning to end. It didn't suit the dragon a bit!

Then Twinkle hid in a corner to see what the dragon would say. All the pink would easily wash off, so, after the first shock, perhaps the dragon would laugh and think Twinkle was a daring elf.

But, dear me, goodness gracious, buttons and buttercups, stars and moon! The dragon didn't think it was funny, or daring, or clever, or anything else! As soon as he woke up and saw his pink geese, his pink-tailed and pink-whiskered cat, and his own terrible pink tail, he flew into the most dreadful rage that was ever seen!

He roared so loudly that the mountain not far away had its top broken off with the shock. He blew out so much smoke that everyone for miles around wondered where the thick fog came from. He shot flames from his mouth and very nearly burned up his cave, his geese, his cat, himself and poor, frightened Twinkle!

That silly little elf was really almost scared out of his skin. Who would have thought that Snorty would make such a fuss! Goodness gracious! Snorty roared again, and blew out more smoke. Then he began to look for that naughty little Twinkle. Twinkle saw two great red eyes like engine-lamps coming towards him, and he picked up his pot of paint and fled!

How he ran! How he flew! How he jumped and bounded and skipped! And after him galloped Snorty the Dragon, smoke and flames flying behind him and terrible roars filling the air. Right through Fairyland they went, the two of them, for Twinkle didn't dare to stop for a minute.

At last the elf came to the gate of Fairyland itself, and he flew over it. The dragon came up to the gate and roared to the gate-keeper to open it for him – but the pixie shook his head.

'No dragons allowed out of Fairyland,' he said.

'Very well, then, I shall sit here and wait for Twinkle to come back,' roared the dragon, and down he sat, just inside the gate. And there he is still, waiting for the elf to come creeping back again.

But Twinkle is afraid to go back. So he lives in our world now, and he is really quite happy, using his paint and paintbrush all the year round. And what do you think he does? You have often seen his work, though you may not have known it. He paints the tips of the little white daisies on our lawns and in our fields! Go and look for them – you are sure to find a pretty, pink-tipped one. Then you will know that that mischievous elf, Twinkle, is *some*where near. Call him and see if he comes!

How Untidy!

There were once some small brownies who lived in tiny houses at the end of Cherry Wood. They were cheerful, merry little creatures, but how untidy!

Really, you could hardly get into their houses for the mess and muddle they were in! The mats were crooked and needed beating, the curtains were in rags, the chimneys smoked, and every brownie looked as if he could do with a good wash and brush up.

'How untidy!' said the fairies, going by with their noses in the air.

'How untidy!' said the rabbits in disgust.

'How untidy!' said the Fairy Queen herself, as she drove through Cherry Wood and saw the houses of the small brownies. She stopped her carriage and got out.

'Come here,' she said to the scared brownies. 'How dare you keep your houses in such a mess! Now listen to me – if you don't keep them more tidy I shall send old Witch Stamparound to look after you, and you won't like *her*, I can tell you!'

'Oh, please, please, no,' said the brownies, who knew that Witch Stamparound was a terribly strict person.

But they didn't become any more tidy, and one day old Witch Stamparound did arrive! Goodness, you should have seen her! She wore six pairs of spectacles, the better to see any speck of dirt, and her nose was all wrinkled through being turned up in disgust at dirtiness and untidiness!

She set to work to make those brownies tidy. She scolded them, she made them wash, brush, clean, and scrub all day long and sometimes half the night too. They couldn't bear it, and were very unhappy.

'Let's run away!' whispered one.

'She would catch us!' said another.

'Well, let's *fly* away!' said a third.

'That's a good idea,' said the first one. 'The old witch only has her broomstick to fly on. We'll hide that, then she won't be able to chase us.'

'We haven't any wings, so we had better change ourselves into little brown birds,' said the biggest brownie. 'I've got a bird spell some-where.'

He hunted for it and found it in a dusty drawer. It was a box of tiny yellow pills.

'Where are the spells that will change us back to our own shape?' asked the smallest brownie.

'I've got them safely in my pocket,' said the biggest brownie. 'Now come along, everyone – here's a yellow pill for each of you. As soon as you've swallowed it you'll turn into birds. Spread your wings and fly away. I've hidden the old witch's broomstick!'

They swallowed the pills, and hey presto! each brownie became a small bird, dressed in brown feathers the same colour as their suits had been. They spread their wings and flew away, and although the old witch shouted after them she could not stop them, for she could not find her broomstick anywhere!

But what a dreadful thing – when they arrived at a wood far away, where they would be safe, the biggest brownie, who was now the biggest sparrow, couldn't find the spells to change them back into brownies again. You see, he now had no pockets for he was dressed in feathers, and no matter how he hunted, the pills to change them back again were quite gone!

So little brown birds they had to remain – and they are with us still. You know the sparrows, don't you? How they chatter and chirp, and how they love to come round our houses to be with us!

But, you know, they are still terribly untidy! Have you seen their nests? Go and look for one this year, tucked away somewhere under the eaves, in a gutter pipe. Then you will see how untidy those small brownies are still! Pieces of straw hang down here and there, and the nests really look as if they will fall to bits! And you will say, as the Fairy Queen said about their houses long ago, 'HOW UNTIDY!'

Three Cheers for John!

At John's school they did a great many exciting things in nature lessons. They grew seeds, they kept caterpillars, and there was a big aquarium tank, too, where two little sticklebacks were making a nest. John loved the nature lesson, and he was always going out for walks to find flowers or to watch the birds building their nests and fetching grubs for their little ones.

One child each week took the caterpillars home at the weekend to look after them, for they could not be left on the classroom windowsill from Friday to Monday. John had had his turn, and dear me, the teacher thought they had grown twice as large in John's care! He was very good with everything alive, big or little.

This week it was Billy's turn. He was a careless little boy, and the teacher spoke to him sharply.

'Now, Billy, it's your turn to take the

caterpillars home this weekend and feed them and clean out their box. See you do it well, for they are growing big now and will soon turn into chrysalides.'

'Yes, Miss Brown,' said Billy.

But do you know, he forgot all about taking them home that Friday afternoon! A circus was coming to their village, and all the children were so eager to see it coming through the streets that everyone rushed off and nobody thought of the caterpillars at all. Even the teacher forgot, for it was prize-giving day on Monday, and she was busy arranging all the prizes and putting out the little silver mugs and cups that had been won at the sports by the children. There was a lot to do. She arranged all the things on a table, ready for the parents to see, and went home.

Billy didn't think about the caterpillars that night, nor all the next day, which was Saturday – but John did. He wondered if Billy was treating the little things properly, for he quite thought that Billy had taken them home. So he went round to Billy's house to ask him if the caterpillars were all right.

'Ooh, my!' said Billy, at once. 'I forgot to bring them home!'

'Forgot to bring them home!' said John, in

dismay. 'Oh, poor things! Their leaves will be dead, and they won't have anything to eat. I do think you are unkind, Billy.'

'Well, I can't help it, I'm not going to bother about them now,' said Billy sulkily.

'You ought to go and get the key from the caretaker, next door to the school, and fetch them home,' said John. 'They will die.'

'Well, let them!' said Billy unkindly. 'They are only caterpillars.'

'I don't like you, Billy,' said John in disgust, and he turned away to go home. But those caterpillars worried him. He couldn't bear to think of them dying because their leaves were dead and dry. He wondered what to do. He was going to the circus that night – perhaps he could leave early, get the key from old Mrs White and fetch the caterpillars home himself. He could feed and clean them that night and they would be all right. If they were left till the next day they would certainly die.

So he went to the circus with the others, and slipped away before it was finished, though he badly wanted to see the end of it; but he was afraid that old Mrs White would have gone to bed if he got to her house too late.

But dear me, when he did get there, there was

no answer! The old lady had gone away for the weekend and her house was empty. Now what was John to do? There didn't seem anything to be done at all!

'I'll just go and peep in at the schoolroom window,' thought John. 'I've got my torch with me and I can shine it down on the caterpillar box and see if they are all right or not.' So he went round to the school and walked over to the window.

Then he stopped in the greatest surprise – for there was someone in the classroom – someone with a torch that shone on to the prizes all so neatly arranged on the table. And that someone had come to steal the silver cups!

John crept away from the window and ran to the police station. 'There's a burglar in my classroom at the school!' he cried. 'Quick, sir, he's stealing all our prizes!'

The policeman put on his coat and came at once – and he was just in time to catch the thief as he climbed out of the window with his bag full of the silver cups and other prizes! He was taken to the police station and locked up.

John didn't forget the caterpillars in his excitement. No, he went back to the school, took the box of caterpillars from the open window, shut the window down and went home. He cleaned out the box before he went to bed and gave the poor caterpillars some fresh leaves, for they looked ill and feeble. The next day they were perfectly all right again.

John took them back to school on Monday, and the teacher didn't notice that it was John who brought them back and not Billy. Billy looked ashamed of himself, and thanked John in a whisper – but John wouldn't smile at him. He thought Billy was mean and unkind.

What a surprise at prize-giving time! In the middle of it, when all the parents were sitting watching the boys and girls go up for their prizes, the policeman walked in and spoke to the headmaster. Then he handed a little parcel to him and went out.

The headmaster turned to the waiting people. 'You have all heard,' he began, 'how the prizes were nearly stolen from us on Saturday night and how John Watson helped the police to catch the thief and give us back our prizes. I should like to say that the reason John was here that night so late was because, being a kind-hearted lad, he had remembered that the caterpillars in his classroom had not been taken home that weekend by the boy who should have looked

after them – and John had come to see if they
were all right. That was how he saw the thief.
The police are delighted to have caught the
man, as they have been after him for some time
– and as a reward to John they have sent him
this silver watch – which I now present to you,
John, with my best wishes and thanks to you for
saving our prizes!'

John came up, blushing bright red.

'I am also pleased to say that John wins the
nature prize,' said the headmaster, and gave
John – what do you think? – a little camera!
John was so delighted that he could hardly say
thank you.

'Now what about three cheers for the boy who
came to find the caterpillars and caught a
burglar instead?' smiled the headmaster. 'If it
had not been for John we should none of us have
been here at a prize-giving today – for there
would have been no prizes. Now then, all
together – hip, hip, hurrah! Three cheers for
John!'

'Hip, hip, hurrah!' shouted everyone. John
was proud and happy – and there was only
one person there who was even prouder and
happier. His mother!

Cuckoo!

Winnie and Tony were playing in the woods together. They had kept houses, played school and had hunted for primroses. Now Winnie was tired and wanted to go home.

'*I'm* not tired!' said Tony. 'I'd like a game of hide-and-seek.'

'I don't want to play,' said Winnie. 'You stay here if you like. I'm going home. I'll tell Mummy you'll come soon.'

Off she went, and Tony was left alone in the wood, halfway up a tree he was climbing.

'Winnie's silly!' he grumbled to himself. 'She might have stayed and had a game. I love hide-and-seek!'

As he was climbing down the tree someone called, 'Cuckoo! Cuckoo!'

'Good old Winnie!' said Tony, pleased. 'She is playing after all! I suppose she found a good hiding place as she ran off, and hid there. All right, Winnie! I'll find you!'

He ran towards the voice and hunted through the bushes. 'Where are you?' he cried.

'Cuckoo! Cuckoo!' came the voice, this time behind him. Tony ran off again, looking behind the trees and under the bushes. Wherever could Winnie be?

'Call again!' he shouted. No answer. Then, after a while, he heard once more: 'Cuckoo!'

'Well, where *are* you?' cried Tony, crossly. 'You're not to dodge about like that, Winnie. Keep in one place. It isn't fair.'

'Cuckoo, cuckoo, cuckoo!' This time it was to the left of him, quite near. Tony felt really cross. Winnie wasn't playing fair. She wasn't hiding in the same place all the time. She was creeping round about him.

'I give up!' he cried. 'Where are you, Winnie? Come out and show me!'

'Cuckoo! Cuckoo!'

'Don't be silly, I'm not playing any more!' shouted Tony. 'Come out, Winnie, and we'll go home together.'

But Winnie didn't come out. Nobody came at all – but still someone called: 'Cuckoo! Cuckoo!'

'All right, then, silly, I'm going home by myself!' said Tony in a huff, and he ran home.

But Winnie was there before him! She opened the door to him!

'How did you get here so soon?' said Tony in surprise. 'You might have told me where you were hiding, Winnie. I looked and looked and looked.'

'But I didn't play hide-and-seek,' said Winnie in astonishment. 'I came straight home. I've been helping Mummy get the tea for ever so long.'

'You couldn't have been,' said Tony. 'Because I kept hearing you call "Cuckoo", Winnie.'

'I didn't,' said Winnie.

'You did!'

'I didn't!'

'You did!'

'Children, children, don't quarrel!' called their mother. 'Tony, you're a silly boy. Listen at the front door for a minute.'

Tony went there and listened – and from the woods came a call: 'Cuckoo! Cuckoo!'

'Oh!' said Tony, going red. 'It's the cuckoo come back to us again after being away all the winter. Oh, what a silly I am! I played hide-and-seek with him!'

And how Mummy and Winnie laughed!

Enid Blyton

SEVEN O'CLOCK TALES

'Wait! Wait!' John cried. 'I could take you to your party! I could put you all into my new basket!'

An enchanting collection of nearly thirty stories. There's the mischievous shoemaker who sews a Skippetty Spell into the King's shoes, a pixie who finds a magic shoelace which grants his every wish, a basketful of brownies on their way to a Fairyland party – and much, much more!

Enid Blyton

EIGHT O'CLOCK TALES

'Who are you? Where do you come from?' the pixie children cried in excitement.

A delightful collection of adventures in which a brave scarecrow foils a plot to kidnap Princess Peronel, two naughty children eat some magic shrinking sweets, and Mollie pays a visit to the old woman who lives in a Shoe, and who makes her doll come to life!